The Great Chicago Fire

(A LOVE STORY)

by Elizabeth Massie

Ardie charged, bellowing, and Russell jumped out of the way in time to send Ardie in a stagger. Russell grabbed up a broken beam lying at the side of the alley and, gripping one end, swung it hard, aiming for Ardie's shoulders. He caught the man solidly in the back. Ardie croaked and fell to the ground, striking his head on the ground.

"I won!" shouted Russell, spinning to face John. "Not a cut on me."

"But Ardie's not dead!" John yelled.

"I didn't say I'd kill him, just beat him."

"Get up, Ardie!" said John. "Don't lose my bet!"

"Get up, Ardie!" said Russell. "We have to get away, and now or we'll all die!"

Ardie groaned but didn't get up.

Thank God! Russell won the bet! Katina thought. She wanted to run to him but Madame Jocelyn pulled her back. "Let's *go*! I don't want to burn to death! Russell will join us!" the old woman yelled.

Russell grabbed Ardie's arm but the man lay, unable to move. "John, help me! We have to get him up! We have to go!"

But John pointed his pistol at Russell. "Kill him or I'll kill you!"

Russell dropped Ardie's arm. "No!"

"Do it!" demanded John.

And at that moment, with a deafening crack, the rotted, burning tenement gave way, the remainder of its roof falling in on itself and the outer wall falling with a roar and a fiery crash onto the alley and on top of Russell and Ardie.

ISBN 978-1-63789-817-8
"Originally published as The Great Chicago Fire: 1871,
by Archway Paperback, Pocket Books 1999

For information address Crossroad Press at 141 Brayden Dr., Hertford, NC 27944
A Rendezvous Press Production
Rendezvous Press is an imprint of Crossroad Press.
www.crossroadpress.com

Crossroad Press Trade Edition

1

Chief Jones Share System, Pies, With Boston Fire Department Officials

Visitors from Boston, including fire department officials and city councilmen, arrived in Chicago yesterday afternoon for the purpose of examining the workings of our city's renovated fire-alarm system. Boston's fire department spokesman Leon Briscoe stated their business as gathering information on how they could improve their own systems at home.

"Our method for protecting the citizens of this fair city is the best in the country," Chief Fire Marshal Robert A. Jones told the Bostonians, describing the network which keeps the city informed and abreast of blazes in order to stop them before major damage can occur. "Not even New York can boast of a more proficient system for detecting and halting fires. The Queen of the West leads the way yet again. We have seventeen steam-driven fire engines, two hose elevators, four hook-and-ladder wagons, and twenty-three hose carts. I challenge you to find a more complete array in any American city!"

The entourage visited the courthouse where they were treated to a lunch of pork, breads, and rhubarb pie, supplied by Mrs. Jones and a friend, Mrs. Samuel Johnson. The visiting team was then escorted up the narrow steps of the 100-foot-tall cupola, where Chicago watchmen faithfully scan the city 24 hours a day from the walkway outside the top of the tower.

"Each neighborhood has an alarm box mounted in a prominent place," Marshal Jones continued as the amazed Bostonians cautiously peered over the edge of the walkway, gazing out at the rooftops of Chicago, "usually on a storefront. These boxes are numbered, according to their location. If a fire is spotted by the neighborhood watch or by some common citizen, he telegraphs the courthouse, using a number to designate the area of the city in which the fire was discovered. If a watchman in the tower spies smoke or flames, they likewise alert the fire houses in the vicinity of the fire. For added security, we also have the courthouse bell, which is quite loud, and when it is rung alerts the citizens of the danger of fire." For added emphasis, Marshal Jones had the watchmen on duty ring the bell once, causing the visitors to cover their ears.

One Boston official, Jeffrey van Hozier, pointed out that he'd seen one of the alarm boxes on a stroll earlier, nailed to the outside of a barbershop, and was surprised to find it was locked. Marshal Jones explained simply that this prevented false alarms. "The keys to the boxes are kept by trustworthy citizens who live nearby." After returning to the main floor of the courthouse, Mr. Briscoe asked, "Do you believe then, that fire is no longer a threat to Chicago?"

To which Marshal Jones answered, "Fire will always be a concern. I would be a fool to think otherwise. But with our system of detecting and fighting blazes, I must say that we have never encountered a fire we could not control, and I cannot imagine that we will. The citizens of

Chicago are in good hands and can rest easy."

George Rainey, *Chicago Tribune*
June 2, 1871

The applause from the audience was greater than the size of the audience warranted. With only sixteen people and their thirty-two hands, Katina Monroe would have thought the response to the final act of *Men and the Sky* would have barely been enough to stir the dust in the rafters or flicker the lights of the kerosene lanterns. But the men and women who had come to opening night and had dropped their meager donations into the jar by the door were thrilled with the story of two boys who grow up and, with the help of a magical bird, build a kingdom in the clouds. And now, as the four actors took their bows, some members of the audience called out "Bravo! Bravo!"

Katina bowed deeply from the waist. Next to her, lanky Adam MacPherson, her fellow actor, bowed,whispering, "Author, author! You'll be our century's Shakespeare!"

"Ha!" Katina said softly. "I don't think the Bard and I have much in common, other than a love of words and fantasy. My stories are not poetic, but simple."

"Our audiences understand the simple," said Adam. "The rag collector, the knife grinder. They're the ones clapping, my friend."

Katina glanced at him as she bent forward again and gave him a grin. Her heart pounded with the excitement of victory. *If moments like this could last forever,* she thought, *then I could forget the terrible things that have happened to me over the past years.*

After another few moments of bows, the other two actors, Chadwick Tomms and Pip Harrison, stepped to the side of the stage, took the curtains—worn, paper-thin bed linens—and tugged them closed along the tight line of hemp rope. The applause began to fade. The actors grabbed each other in rough and cheerful hugs.

"Bravo, indeed!" said Chadwick, at twenty the oldest of the troupe. His sandy hair stood up, matted with sweat. "I can't believe I remembered all those lines."

"Aye," said curly-haired Pip, nineteen, his accent thick with the Scottish countryside from which he'd come to Chicago five years earlier. "And I fed ya nearly a third of those lines from behind me hand. Yer brain's a sieve! Look on the floor there and I think that's where most of those forgotten lines ran down to!" Chadwick gave Pip a hearty shove and they both laughed.

"Give the folks a few moments to clear the place," said Chadwick, shedding the woolen cape and tin crown that were part of his costume, "and we'll close up and go back to my flat. I've some stale gingerbread cake given me by Patterson, and some ale to top it off. My mother works at the stockyard until midnight, so we'll have the place to ourselves for two hours."

"So be it!" said Adam.

"Cake it is!" said Pip.

Katina adjusted the black felt hat on her head and smiled but said nothing. She knew she wouldn't go to Chadwick's flat for talk and cake. It wouldn't be appropriate.

Suddenly, two grinning faces appeared through the curtains. Becky Alaimo, a skinny red-haired girl with a mangled ear, and Alice Montague, a sweet chubby girl with two front teeth missing, giggled and invited the actors to come to their place of employment, the Stick Saloon on Quincy Street.

"Why don't you follow us back to work?" asked Alice, tossing her head so hard the red cap pinned to her straw-colored hair nearly flopped off. Her words hissed because of the missing teeth. "We're due there now. We've music, dancin', and entertainment! We'll even treat you to a free beer, first time."

Katina spoke quickly. "Thank you, but we have other plans, play notes and the like. Don't we, fellows?"

Becky's laugh was more like a bark. "Listen to the child! You's all such babies. Pity. Come, on Alice. They'll stop by when they grow up."

The girls' heads withdrew and their shrill laughter trailed them all the way out the stable door.

Chadwick rubbed at something in his eye. "We may not have play notes," he said. "But I'll be hanged before I'd step inside the Stick. They're as likely to rob you as entertain you. I'd rather take my chances on the streets."

Adam and Pip nodded in agreement.

There wasn't much to close up the theater at the end of a show. Katina swept the stage and the wooden floor between the benches, showing out clumps of dried mud, while Pip returned the props to the prop box, Chadwick latched the windows, and Adam sat on the floor in what had once been a feed stall and sorted the coins from the donation jar by the light of a lantern.

MacPherson Theater was a converted stable, owned by Adam's father, Sanford. Sanford had gone west to seek his fortune with his wife and seven youngest MacPherson children, and Adam had promised to keep the stable in business. Three months after his family had left, the stable was still in business but there was not a horse nor bit of tack in the place. Adam had cleaned it out, laid a wood floor, build a stage, constructed ten crude benches and sanded them down so a lady would not catch a splinter in her backside, and then put the word out that he was going to produce plays. It had been in business now for almost a year.

Katina had met Adam at Anderson's Market on Fourth Avenue, where she ran errands and unloaded wagons. Adam shopped at Anderson's on Wednesdays, and when he had mentioned his new theater, Katina admitted she'd written a play called *Fancy and the Captain,* about a silly young woman pining over a haughty sea caption. Adam asked to see it and was so impressed that it became the second production ever held in his theater. Katina quickly composed a second play in her hours after work, *Little Man of the Mountain,* a story of a forgetful gnome. This, too, had been performed on the stable's stage to the admiration of the residents of the destitute neighborhood.

The stable-turned-theater made no money compared to the stable as stable, but Adam loved performing so much it didn't matter. He earned his bread and butter as a carpenter's helper for a man named Simple Parker, mainly laying down planks for sidewalks in the business district of South Division just a few blocks northeast; Pip was employed at the gasworks on Monroe and Chadwick, manned the ovens at Patterson's bakery.

When the worse of the mud had been chased outside, Katina

extinguished all but three lanterns and brought them back to the stall where Adam had been joined by Chadwick and Pip. The three were sitting in a circle, shirts off, wiping their chests.

"Just enough to pay for kerosene for the next few Saturday nights and for each of us to have a few pennies," Adam told Katina as she sat down.

"Let's put our money together to have a new curtain sewn," said Pip.

"Ah, what this theater needs in a lady's touch," said Chadwick. "None of us can thread a needle. Our costumes are naught but our own clothes, decorated with a stray bit of tin or tassel."

Adam shook his head. "A lady would only whine and complain that the theater is too shabby, the stage too rough, the kerosene too smoky. No, an all-man troupe is what I have and what I shall continue to have."

Katina crossed her arms. This conversation had come up before. There were always rips in costumes needing mending, or a female character who might have been more accurately played by a girl than a boy in girl's clothing. But Adam said keeping women out of his productions had not hurt Shakespeare. Adam would never let a woman get involved in his theater. And as far as he knew, there were no females in his theater troupe.

Adam hopped up and dropped the coins into the pocket of his trousers. He shoved one sleeve of his damp shirt into his waistband then slipped his tattered wool jacket on over bare skin. "I'll concede one thing," he said. "When we've earned a good reputation and the rich have discovered our whereabouts, and when we are earning as much as the Steward Grand Theatre or Crosby's Opera House, then perhaps we share hire a costume maker. But she would be paid to work and keep her thoughts to herself."

"Here, here!" said Chadwick. "To the time we are as well-respected as the Grand Theatre!"

The actors collected their lanterns and went outside. The June night air was beginning to mist over with an impending shower, and the road was rutted and muddy. Through the open windows of the four-story tenement across Fifth Avenue came the sounds of babies crying, men shouting, women yelling. From north and south along the road came other sounds—singing, fighting, a fiddle scratching out an unrecognizable tune, doors slamming. It was a usual Saturday night with usual Saturday night noises.

Adam and Chadwick locked the stable door and tugged it to make sure it was secured. There were child gangs and dangerous men who prowled the streets of this neighborhood, and one couldn't take chances without a strong lock. The gangs were out at all hours of the night, knocking folks senseless to steal watches, money, or anything else of interest. Although the people of this neighborhood had little worth stealing, that didn't matter to the thieves. During the day they worked alone in the fashionable business districts several blocks over, picking the pockets of the gentlemen and ladies, but at night they'd gather together, get drunk and angry, tune turn their energies against their own people on their own streets.

"There," said Adam, turning from the locked door. "And now we're off to Chadwick's for refreshments."

"Except for me," said Katina.

They'd heard this before. "What is it with writers?" declared Pip. "Ye's been part of this troupe long as the rest of us yet you've never gone out with us for a bit o' fun. Do ye dislike our company so much?"

"Do we bore you?" asked Chadwick. "Do we stink?"

Katina shook her head. "I'm tuckered, is all. I would fall asleep with a mug in my hand and spill ale on Chadwick's mother's fine carpet."

"Fine carpet!" chuckled Chadwick. "Oh, that we have!"

"Come with us, please?" asked Adam.

"I need my sleep," said Katina. "Because tomorrow I shall begin writing yet another play, one even better than *Men and the Sky*."

Adam shook his head and squinted at her. It wasn't just poor light that made him do so. He had poor eyesight and was in great need of spectacles, which he could not afford. "Writers. A peculiar bunch if ever there was one. But remember, we'll practice Thursday night. The play went well but there are always improvements that can be made."

Katina nodded. She could feel the first drops of rain plop onto her cap and run down the sides of her face. Her auburn hair, cut as short as Adam's and Chadwick's, was beginning to curl with the damp.

"You want us to walk you home?" asked Pip.

"Don't worry about me, I'll be fine," said Katina. "Robbers don't like the rain. They'll be finding shelter at a saloon or in the tunnels beneath the buildings of Conley's Patch 'til the worst is over."

"Suit yourself," said Adam. "Watch out for the road mud, though. I heard that after the rain last week, somebody down on Third Avenue found a brand new hat lying on the street, only to pick it up and discover there was a man underneath. They asked the man wasn't he glad he'd been found? He said yes, but the horse he was riding was still holding its breath."

"Ah!" Katina laughed and swung her lantern, catching Adam in the back with it as the others moved off. "You had me believing for a moment."

Holding her lantern out before her, Katina walked to the end of Fifth Avenue and turned west on Quincy by Sallee's Butcher Shop, watching her steps. The story of the man and the horse might be farce, but she'd lost a shoe in the mud not long ago and had to pry it out with the sturdy stick she kept in her back pocket for protection. But there was one consolation: she wore men's clothes, and they didn't require hands to clutch her skirts to keep her hems from dragging on the sorry surface of the road.

"William!" shouted Adam from the corner.

Katina turned around.

"You said earlier that you and the Bard have little in common. But think! You share a first name!"

"That we do," said Katina.

And the three other actors turned away, their lanterns bobbing, scattering shadows across the road and the side of a slowly passing wagon.

William, thought Katina. That's me. *Although I'm eighteen-year-old Katina Monroe, no one in Chicago knows who I truly am. They all think I'm fifteen-year-old William Monroe.*

The tenement in which she lived was two blocks up then down a wide, rutted stretch people referred to as Rat's Alley. Unlike the fancy mansions along Lake Michigan to the east, or the newer homes across the Chicago River to the north, this district was the bane of the city, rundown and dangerous, lined with degrading shops, shanties, and rickety tenement buildings. Katina hadn't known how bad it was when she had come here from Georgia. All she knew was that she needed a place she could afford, a place where she could forget the past eight years of her life.

The rain began to pick up. The steady patter soaked Katina's coat and trousers. She tried to walk faster but the mud sucked at her shoes and made progress difficult. On both sides of the street, late-night gamblers and drinkers withdrew into their dimly lit shelters to continue their merrymaking. Others hid out in the cavernous, musky tunnels and makeshift rooms beneath the buildings which had been raised as part of the city's ongoing renovation, but had not yet been filled in with soil or rock. Inside the Stick Saloon, someone was pounding out "Rain on the Lilacs" on a badly-tuned piano.

Gritting her teeth, Katina hurried as best she could. At home, she would light the stove and dry her clothes. She didn't really plan on writing tonight. Her thoughts were fuzzy with fatigue. She just couldn't take a chance spending extra time with her friends from the theater for fear they might discover her true identity. Although they were the closest friends she had, she didn't trust them completely.

Nobody could be trusted completely. It was a hard fact of life.

She reached the middle of the block and turned north into Rat's Alley. Katina's boarding house was near the end, just past a pile of blackened beams that had been a garment factory before it burned in November. The residents of the alley had made the scorched hull a dumping ground for rubbish—rotted food, bones and gristle, splintered wood scraps, open paper, shattered bottles. The place stank worse than the Chicago River, but at least on a rainy night the smell was reduced. Katina held her lantern high and the light splashed against the buildings on both side of the alley.

A cup of tea will warm my mind and ease my stomach. What I wouldn't give to be able to have some of Chadwick's cake. How I miss good food, a comfortable house, clean closes, someone to share my home and meals and conversation. How I miss family—

Something struck her from behind, so hard that her lantern flew from her hand and she fell face down on the muddy alleyway. Grit and gravel filled her mouth. "Oww!" she cried, instantly rolling over on her back to see what was after her.

Standing over her was a blond boy, no more than eight or nine, wielding a large metal pipe in his hand. He was dressed in knee pants, a coat way too large for him, and a smashed top hat.

"Gimme what ya got," demanded the child.

Katina had learned to fight here in Chicago, something she'd never imagined she would do back in Georgia. In this city, however, it was a skill she had to have. *I should have let Adam and the others walk me home,* she thought, reaching for the stick in her back pocket. *This boy would not have challenged the four of us!*

"I haven't anything," said Katina as she carefully pulled herself to her feet. Her back stung fiercely but she would worry about that later. She held the stick behind her. She didn't want to strike him or make him think she would. She knew these children; if they felt threatened, they could become even more violent. They stick was a last resort. "Go on, or I'll call for the authorities."

"Authorities!" said the boy. He spit on the road. "Authorities don't care to be here in Rat's Alley. Besides, the men here pay them to stay away. Now, empty your pockets or you'll have the end of this rod again."

Katina knew getting away was better than confrontation. She'd learned to fight, yes, but she was not very skilled if surprise was not on her side. She slowly began to back up. On the road nearby lay her lantern, the globe cracked but not broken, sending a pool of light across the uneven ground. Several women, huddled beneath shawls, passed by on the other side of the alley but didn't look her way.

"Go on," Katina said to the boy. "I've got nothing."

"You do," said the boy. "I don't wanna hit you again, but I will!" He took several steps forward, the pipe shaking in his grasp.

The crumpled remains of the old furniture factory was right there. The boy might be younger, but Katina had longer legs. She could jump through the rubbish pile if lucky and he would have to crawl over it. She could then kick a pile down on him and escape out the other side.

The boy waved the pipe. "Give me!"

Katina spun about and dashed for the rubbish.

"Come back!"

She reached the pile and tried to stretch her legs enough to hurdle it, but her foot slipped in the mud and she crashed into it. Her cheeks were sliced by glass shards and the palms of her hands were cut by exposed nails. Her foot caught in a tangle of wires. Her protection stick was knocked form her hand and sent skittering away in the rain.

He's going to hit me! She thought, closing her eyes and raising her hands to protect her head. She gritted her teeth and prepared for the blow.

2

The blow didn't come. She counted her breaths. *One, two, three, four, five.* She could hear a dog somewhere far down the alley, howling at real or imaginary prey. Six, seven, eight…

She opened her eyes. Her heart continued to thunder.

Nine? Ten?

The boy was still in the middle of the alley, and a tall man stood before him. The man was not easy to distinguish because of the rain and the night, but one hand was clearly pointing at the boy. The boy was looking down, the pipe still in his fist.

"Bruce," said the man at last. "What are you doing? You promised me."

The boy said nothing. He rubbed water from the bridge of his nose.

"Bruce!"

"What?"

"Give me the pipe and help me get that poor boy out of the rubbish."

The boy grunted but handed over the pipe. The man stuck it into the pocket of his long canvas coat, picked up Katina's cracked lantern, and took the boy by the shoulder. The boy grimaced but didn't pull away. Together they came up to where Katina was sprawled in the garbage, rain and tickles of blood running down her face.

The man handed the lantern to Katina. In its light, she could see his face more clearly. He was not much older than she, perhaps nineteen or twenty. He was as tall as Adam, but much more striking, with brown hair and blue eyes shaded by heavy brows. His nose was straight and prominent. His voice was confident, bearing traces of an education most people in this neighborhood did not have. Katina felt her mouth go dry in embarrassment. She wished she had not met this handsome young man in this way.

"Are you hurt?" he asked. "Here." He held out his hand and Katina took it. She winced slightly, silently, with the pain. With an easy move, he lifted her to her feet, where she stood wobbling slightly. The boy stared at his toes.

"You are hurt," the man said. "Ah, look at all this." He gently reached out and flicked pieces of glass from Katina's face. "The cuts aren't deep, though. That's good. Can you walk?"

Katina nodded.

"Bruce," said the man. "What should you do now besides stand there like a horse swishing away flies?"

The boy shrugged.

"Apologize," said the man.

The boy kicked the ground and said, "Sorry."

"And offer to help me show this boy to his home."

Bruce frowned. "I don't want to."

"We had an understanding, Bruce. Are you going to break your word to me?"

The boy slowly shook his head.

"Very well, then," said the man. Then he turned to Katina. His smile was genuine and warm. "My name is Russell Cosgrove. This is Master Bruce Charles. We are friends, and we look out for each other, don't we, Bruce?"

Bruce muttered, "Yes."

"And you are?" asked the man.

"William Monroe," said Katina, and the words raked her throat like the glass has raked her flesh. If only she could tell Russell Cosgrove the truth. If only he could know that she was not a young boy at all, but a young woman. She couldn't, of course. To destroy her disguise now would be to throw her entire life into a terrible spiral that she didn't want to consider.

Russell touched her face one last time, searching for glass, and then he let go. The warmth from his touch lingered on her cheeks as a blush. Surprised and embarrassed, she turned away she he wouldn't see.

"Master Monroe," said Russell. "Where do you live, so we can escort you there safely?"

Katina stood as straight as she could. Her knees hurt. There was likely glass there, too, which she would remove at home. "The Brandermill Boarding House. I was nearly home when Bruce attacked me. I don't need assistance, however. Just a promise from that young wolf there that he will leave unsuspecting folks alone."

"Are you certain?" asked Russell.

"Certainly, I'm certain," said Katina. Her curious interest in this man was fading, to be replace by growing anger. *Why is he being kind to that ruffian? The boy should be punished for such behavior. He should be locked up in jail with all the other criminals who roam the streets at night.*

"Then have a good evening, Master Monroe," said Russell.

"Good evening," mumbled Katina. She turned on her heel and, ignoring the ache in her legs and back, snatched up her safety stick and strode with head held high to the porch of the boardinghouse. She didn't look back until she was on the top step, and only then to take a quick peek. Russell Cosgrove and Bruce Charles were no longer in the rainy alley.

Room 305 was on the third floor, up two flights of rickety stairs and past many other flats, their doors locked against the nighttime. Mrs. Brandermill, the landlady, stuck her head out her door as Katina passed, her pretty, delicate face obscured in shadow. She whispered, "How did your play go, William? Oh, I wish I could have seen it!"

Katina smiled and said, "We were simply stupendous."

Mrs. Brandermill nodded. "Someday I will come watch, just you wait. And I do look forward to it."

Suddenly, Mr. Brandermill's furious, greasy-bearded face appeared above his wife's. Mrs. Brandermill withdrew and the man shouted after her, "Meg, get back to the kitchen before I show you what's what!" And to Katina he growled, "Leave my wife alone, boy. Get your sorry self away from here and back to your room, or you'll feel the wrath of my fist!"

Katina liked Mrs. Brandermill but hated her husband, John. Meg Brandermill was young and five months pregnant with her first child. But John Brandermill was an old man, a gambler and a liar, and he treated his wife like an angry parent treats a child.

The situation made Katina's blood boil.

Katina's flat was a single, drafty room with a stove, a bed, a chair, and a window that looked west toward other tenements, grain elevators, and the South Branch of the Chicago River two blocks away. The stove and bed belonged to the Brandermills. Everything else, which was little indeed, belonged to Katina. A small stack of books, a little rectangular table that she'd bought from another tenant, a few cooking pans and utensils, and a scorched brocade satchel that had once been her mother's.

Katina locked her door, set the lantern on the table, and kicked off her shoes. Her stockings were soaked as were her trousers and shirt and wool jacket, and they stank from the rubbish. She shed these and hung them to dry on nails that spotted the wall, then, naked, draped herself in a thin blanket and turned up the wick in the lantern. Unlike Chicago's fancier homes, this boardinghouse had no gas lighting nor heat. The lantern was the only light she had; the stove the only heat.

She sat heavily on the sagging bed mattress and carefully picked the last of the glass bits from her knees. Then she wet a cloth from the water bowl on the table and dabbed her face, hands, and legs. She would be all right. The cuts stung, but none were bad enough to require bandages. She lay down, put her hands to her forehead, and stared at the ceiling.

Then she began to tremble. "I won't cry," she told herself aloud. "I won't cry. I've been through worse. I just won't think about it."

In the room above her, she could hear Mrs. Agee walking her baby. In the room next to her, she could hear Mr. Conlon talking his son out of a bad dream. There were good people in this dreadful neighborhood, many of them. It just seemed that so often the bad outweighed the good.

The lullaby drifted down from upstairs, made more tender by Mrs. Agee's soft Irish accent.

"Gingerbread, sugar cake, licorice, rose,
Ten little fingers and ten little toes,
Blue eyes, pink cheeks, bunting of silk,
Dream thee child of honey and milk."

The was the same lullaby Katina's mother had sung to Katina and her sister so long ago.

So very long ago and far away.

Things had been good for Katina back in Georgia, so long ago. She had been eight years old in early 1861 and living in a pleasant little house on a small farm just outside of Atlanta, Georgia. Her father, Samuel, was a stern yet very successful and sought-after blacksmith. Her mother, Molly, was a gentle soul who managed the farm and home, raising their two daughters, Katina and her younger sister, Katherine, to be fine ladies. There were riverside picnics and apple butter parties, hay rides and quilting bees. The girls took arithmetic and penmanship lessons together under the strict eye of a dour, matronly tutor who came to the farm two days a week. Katina made up little plays and she and Katherine performed them to the delight of her parents. Katina had imagined she would grow up, marry a loving man, raise several smart daughters, and write plays like *Our American Cousin,* which real actors would perform in elegant theaters.

But then Georgia left the Union. And the war came.

Samuel Monroe left his family on his sorrel mare, promising to return in a matter of months once the Confederates had defeated the aggressive Yankees. Katina and Katherine didn't understand the war, knowing only that those who believed in the institution of slavery in the South wanted to be separate from the North so they could continue the practice without interference. The Monroes owned no one. Mrs. Monroe believed the practice of slavery was an abomination. But Samuel felt it was his duty to fight for Georgia even though Katina's mother begged him to stay. With this, the family found itself caught up in it all, and it was terrifying.

Samuel Moore did not come home. The Yankees ripped through Georgia with rifle, torch, and machete. Soldiers plowed to the coast, destroying all in their path. Afterward, renegades had fanned out and burned other places. The Monroe home was destroyed—the family's horses and chickens taken and the crops and house set afire. Even to this day, Katina could hear the cries of her mother and sister, who were trapped and died in the house as Katina, who had been outside in the orchard writing a play, hid up in an oak tree.

There was nothing I could do. There was nothing I could do!

Katina rolled onto her side and looked out the small window of her flat. All she could see were rivulets of rain on the glass and distorted lamplight from the windows of the tenement building behind her own. She did not want to remember what had happened in Georgia, but she did. The memories were living spirits, coming back and tormenting her when she was exhausted or lonely, and least able to deal with them.

The soldiers had left the farm for the road, passing beneath the tree where she hid trembling. She remembered seeing the pen and paper in the grass beneath her and being certain the men would see them, too, and would look up and find her there. She remembered her heartbeats, so loud in her temples and so frantic in her chest that it seemed a miracle that the men couldn't hear them as well. She remembered the laughter of some and how one said they were faring much better since leaving "the Old Bear," and how they would soon be rich men thanks to Southern men who left their wives and properties behind to go to war. Katina had bit her tongue so hard as not to scream, and she had not.

She did not scream as she clung to the scabby branch of the oak and watched the house, blackened and smoldering, fall in on itself. She did not scream after she had picked through the rubble of the house, finding nothing recognizable except for a scorched satchel that belong to her mother. She wandered the road, heading west, having no idea where she was going. Her mind, numbed with shock, kept her from feeling the hunger, the dread, the weakness.

Two days later she was picked up by a pious young couple in a wagon who took her to an orphan asylum sponsored by their parish. Willowbrook, once an elegant boarding school for girls, was now a home for destitute orphans. The old house had survived the war but was a victim of age and disrepair. The poorly shingled roof allowed rainwater to collect in the attic during storms, and the water leaked down onto the girls and boys as they tried to sleep in their cots at night. The cellar, where the garden's yield of potatoes, apples, and onions were stored, was a nesting ground for mice and black widows.

Miss Alethea Innis, the matron of Willowbrook, did not offer the kind of lessons that Katina had had back at the Monroe farm. Instead, the boys and girls of the asylum learned only domestic chores—cooking, mending, sewing, scrubbing, hauling, digging, mucking—all to the tune of Miss Innis's Bible verses and leather riding crop.

Girls fared worse under Miss Innis's eye than boys. The boys were allowed to take the asylum's wagons to nearby farms to sell the vegetables, eggs, and milk. Miss Innis did not strike the boys as severely as she did the girls, and she often chastised the girls with her grim predictions.

"Ah," the old woman would say. "Boys shall grow up and find their way. God made boys to be independent. But you, girls, you've naught to look forward to but a life under the discipline of your husband and master. Get used to the position of your gender."

Boys didn't stay at Willowbrook as long as the girls did; with Miss Innis's help, most of them found jobs or at least the courage to go out on their own by the time they were fifteen. Katina lived at Willowbrook, bleakly counting the days until she turned eighteen and would be put out or took up a position as an assistant matron at the institution, as several other girls had done.

But then, on a night in early December, 1869, two weeks before her birthday, Katina had discovered something that gave her a plan and a flicker of hope, tucked inside the satchel she'd rescued from her home. She had found a pocket within a pocket, and inside that, a short note on a single, age-faded sheet of paper. The return address had been Chicago.

The wind outside Katina's flat shifted, throwing the rain hard against the window glass. Katina wrapped her arms over her face, fighting to keep the tears at bay. Willowbrook and Miss Innis were in the past. She didn't want to remember, but there was nothing she could do to keep the memories away.

She had run away from Willowbrook. Late at night, when

the frosty December moon was full and the sky was speckled with indifferent stars, she had slipped from the dorm window with the satchel. Behind the old mansion, she'd yanked boys clothing down from the clothesline, stuffed the satchel full of apples and pears from the root cellar, climbed over the stone wall, and took the road north. She wasn't sure how far Chicago was, but it didn't matter. She would find it. She was no longer a little orphan girl; she was nearly seventeen. It was time to determine her own fate, no matter how frightening that prospect seemed. An address from a city in the northwest could be her salvation.

Mrs. Bradford Monroe, 1345 S. Michigan Avenue, Chicago, Illinois.

Several miles up the road, as it had begun to sleet, Katina had hidden beneath a bridge and changed into the trousers, shirt, and jacket. Miss Innis always said boys could go places girls could not. Boys were not harassed because of their frailty. Katina had not felt frail that night; beneath a sheen of icy sweat and anxiety, she felt strong. But being thought of as a boy would make traveling easier. She would keep her disguise until she was safe by the warm hearth in the house on Michigan Avenue.

But Chicago was more dangerous than any rural road, and the family living at 1345 South Michigan Avenue had refused to see her. The burly family maid had chased Katina away from the gate, hurling stones and shouting, "Poor folks always lyin' to get a little somethin' that ain't theirs! Be gone, tramp!" Bruised and shaking, Katina found a room to rent in a boardinghouse on Rat's Alley. She cut her hair, continued to dress as a boy, named herself William, and got a job selling *Tribunes* on snowy street corners. *It won't last long, this disguise,* she told herself. *I'll get past that dreadful maid and convince Mr. and Mrs. Bradford Monroe that we are related. Then I can be myself once more. A girl of good and respectable nature.*

Every day for the first two weeks, she trudged the snowy streets to Michigan Avenue to present herself, Katina Monroe, to the people in the elegant house. And every day, the maid would catch her outside the gate and threaten to beat her or have her arrested if she did not go away.

"But I've this address!" she said time and time again. "It was in my mother's satchel! My family was killed in the war, but I'm alive! I'm Katina Monroe! Don't the master and mistress of this house know about me?"

It didn't matter. She was not allowed on the property. She spent her seventeenth birthday, February fifteenth, alone in her drafty room in Brandermill Boarding House, stuffing rags into wall cracks to keep the rats from coming in to share her mattress.

"Enough!" Katina told herself, sitting up abruptly on her bed and clenching her fists. "Nothing will change the past. Only the future can be altered. Now get some sleep. You've got a letter to deliver in the morning."

She blew out the lantern, curled up on the bed, and closed her eyes. At long last, sleep came, and her dreams were of rain and fire and apples rotting on the ground.

3

Russell Cosgrove's home was on the corner of Adams Street and Fifth Avenue, in a sagging two-room apartment over the butcher shop belonging to Lieutenant and Olive Sallee. The Sallees had their quarters in a long, narrow room behind the shop where the meat—sometimes fresh, sometimes rancid—was delivered on Tuesdays and Fridays. Tonight, Lieutenant and Olive were arguing down in the shop, loud enough that Russell could hear Lieutenant accusing Olive of spending too much time visiting her sister and Olive accusing her husband of leaving the back door open long enough for a dog to come inside and run off with a link of sausages.

"Those two have voices shrill enough to shred wallpaper," Russell muttered to himself as he closed the door against the rain. He shed his coat and went through the small front room and into the bedroom, where he poured lukewarm water from a tin pitcher into a washbasin and splashed his face.

It was after midnight, and Russell was exhausted. His feet throbbed from hours of walking and standing, yet the day had been particularly fruitless. He'd spent most of the morning at the office of the *Chicago Tribune* in the city's bustling business district, leaning against a post in the front hall, waiting to speak to a reporter—any reporter—but getting nothing but dour looks from the employees who came and went. He had a story they needed to write, a story the people of the city needed to read, but no one seemed to want it.

"I'm sorry, *sir*," the woman at the front desk had said in a sarcastic tone after he explained his presence for the sixth time, "your so-called *story* would not be of interest to our basic readership. If you want it told, perhaps you should find a printing press of your own and start your own publication." He had left the office after wasting four hours.

I'll get a reporter's attention some way, Russell thought. He wiped his face with a tattered towel then sat down at the tiny desk in the corner of his bedroom and turned up the wick on the lantern. A yellow glow fell over the surface of the desk and across the backs of his chapped hands. He opened his journal, dipped his pen into the well of ink, and began to write an account of the night's confrontation.

"I was on the streets tonight," he wrote. "A rainy night it was, and dark as hell. In Rat's Alley, I found Bruce who had struck an older boy in the back. What do I do about Bruce? After all the time I've spent talking to him, being a friend, sharing meals, thinking I'd convinced him that violence is not an answer, he is still wild."

Russell lifted the pen and looked at what he had written. Every evening since moving into this flat four weeks ago, he'd kept records of all he'd witnessed. He had come to the worst part of town on purpose, to observe, to record. To help.

Russell slammed the pen on the desk and ran his hands through his soaked hair. Bruce had been a terrible disappointment. And there were many other children just like him, and men and women, without hope, without education, without even a sense of safety on their own streets, angry and defensive, unable to see anything beyond the present moment. It was his plan to do something about it, but the puzzle of despair was too much for one person to solve. How could one man accomplish what had to be done? *I need help, but who is there to help me?*

He put his head down on his desk. The rush of the rain outside made him feel more tired. His arm hurt where he'd been cut three nights earlier. He'd been visiting dance halls and saloons, begging for donations to share with the poor, knowing that the people who ran these places were the only ones in the neighborhood with money. Until he could get the attention and concern of Chicago's wealthy, he had to go somewhere. But the saloon owners had laughed him out to the road, saying they had enough to deal with their own worries without adding those of their neighbors.

"You want me to donate to the poor?" one bad-breathed

proprietor had barked in Russell's face after a drunk had slashed Russell in the forearm with a dagger and held him at bay at knifepoint. "Why should I give away anything I worked so bloody hard for? Take your charity requests to the church!"

And so, Russell had bandaged his arm, toughened his resolve, and taken his requests to the church. Seven of them shut their doors in his face, explaining that they performed enough charity as it was by ministering to the souls of the destitute. "It is God's plan that there always be poor," explained one stiff-necked minster named Botkins. "It's a judgment on them and their immoral behaviors. Let it be."

I will not let it be, Russell thought angrily. *I will never let it be.*

There was a letter between the pages of the Bible on his desk, and Russell pull it out and held it up to the lantern light. The envelope was worn from much handling. The sweat-softened note inside, dated two weeks earlier, was from a friend he'd known at Brickmeyer's School, the college he'd attended in northern Chicago before he'd quit and moved to Chicago's poorest slum.

"My dear Russell," the letter began. I've no idea where you are, but I thought that if I got this letter to your parents, they might be kind enough to pass it on to you. How are you? I was dismayed to discover that you have quit Brickmeyer's, disappearing before our very eyes. Such promise you showed to your law studies. Where are you now? New York City? Boston? Or have you decided to take a train across the western plains to search for gold?

"I miss you so very much. Please tell me you left for a good reason, such as the temptation of gold, and not because we were falling in love.

"If this letter finds its way to you, please reply. I have one more year of studies here, and then I plan on opening my own school to educate young ladies. I have the means to open my school wherever I wish, and would not hesitate to follow you where you have gone. I miss you.

"Yours always, Ellen."

Russell ran his thumb over the signature then slipped the note back into the Bible. He leaned back and stared out his window at the rain. Ellen Molloy was a beautiful girl, with hair the color of wheat and eyes as green as Irish shamrocks. She was a year younger than he, and like him, had attended Brickmeyer's College on St. Claire Street. Russell, who had been born and raised in the working class of Chicago's West Side, had saved his money from his work on a grain elevator and enrolled at Brickmeyer's to study to become a lawyer. Ellen Molloy, because of her father's standing in the community and friendship with the headmaster of the school, had been admitted to study where subjects caught her fancy. She was also allowed to have a female chum enroll as well, so she wouldn't be the only woman in attendance. She chose Candace Stephenson, a quiet redhead.

Russell had worked hard the two years he attended the school, absorbing mathematics, law, and, particularly, philosophy and theology. Ellen attended an astronomy class with Russell and they had become good friends. She was smarter than most of the young men at Brickmeyer's. She and Russell spent many hours discussing new medical discoveries, literature, and Russell's evolving ideas about individual value versus collective traditions.

"When one loses his or her freedom for anything short of criminality, it cannot be rationalized that is it for the common good," he had said as they'd sat in the school's side garden in the fall. "Look at the institution of slavery and how it corrupted all involved. No, we as a society owe it to ourselves to protect even the most lowly. It's the only way to keep our honor and moral dignity intact."

"Yet even criminality is constantly redefined," Ellen had said as the leaves from a poplar tree cast swirling shadows on her face. "Some consider it a crime to be poor or uneducated."

Russell nodded. "Some respected religions promote such ideas. But they're wrong. All people are equal, without qualification. Injustice cannot parade as morality, and if I must develop my own theology to be true to what God has put in my heart, I shall do it."

"What would your parents say to such a declaration?"

"I would hope they'd say, 'Godspeed.'"

"Indeed," said Ellen.

That was when Russell, surprising himself, had leaned over and given Ellen a kiss on the cheek. He'd then confided in her that he was from a hard-working but poor family on De Koven Street. He explained that his grandfather had been a Potawatomi warrior—a fact that most well-to-do Chicagoans would have recoiled against—and that the Potawatomis had been forced by government agents to sell their land in 1835 around the village of Chicago so the city could grow. His family understood what it was like to be taken advantage of by the powerful. Ellen seemed neither offended nor shocked. She merely linked her arm in his and said she was glad they were becoming close.

Ellen invited Russell to visit her home in mid-April. Russell did not have enough money for another semester and Ellen assured him her parents would be happy to find a way to help him continue.

The trip to her home was an uncomfortable one for Russell. He had never asked for anything from anybody, but if Ellen's parents were willing to give him the chance to finish his schooling, then he would have to swallow his pride.

The Molloys lived on the North Side, near Lincoln Park, in a large brick house. The opulence of the house made him uneasy and the smooth snobbery of Ellen's parents surprised and angered him. Ellen's mother assured Russell that the Molloy family were not common Irish immigrants such as one would find in the Bohemian shacks on the West Side along with the Germans, Italians, and Scandinavians. The Molloys had been wealthy in Ireland and were wealthy still. Mr. Molloy made his money as a merchant and Mrs. Molloy confided with a smug grin that her home boasted more finery than did her neighbors'.

Russell had sat on the overstuffed chair in the parlor, holding his teacup in his hap, feeling claustrophobic amid the clutter of crystal, porcelain, silver, and lace. It was obvious Ellen had not told her parents that Russell Cosgrove was a poor boy from the West Side, that his family lived in a two-room cottage with a milk cow, and that he had Indian blood in his veins.

The topic of helping Russell finish school never came up.

A little over an hour later, Russell bid a barely controlled farewell then had gone out to the street and yelled. Ellen scurried after him, apologizing, but in that very moment, Russell thought he saw in her eyes a glint of the haughty superiority that had blazed in her mother's. If she'd truly cared about him, she would have told them the truth about him. Maybe he didn't know her at all. Perhaps she had merely found his controversial views entertaining. He realized he could not continue going to Brickmeyer's even if the Molloys somehow gave in and agreed to help pay for his tuition. He couldn't afford more college on his own and he might never be a lawyer, but it didn't take a degree in law to make a difference.

As Ellen stood by the road, Russell had bit her farewell and strode away, never to see her again. He had not returned to school nor to his parents' home on De Koven. He took the little remaining money he'd saved and sought out the most destitute area of the city. An apartment over a butcher shop was all he needed.

He'd spent the following days eating from rubbish dumps, drinking from rain barrels and burst water mains, and praying for guidance.

Here is the problem and here are two hands. What am I to do?

The answer came the following morning while Russell was walking through a filthy alley near Conley's Patch. He found a family of feral cats beneath an empty house, and as he knelt to coax them out, he spied a boy there as well. The boy snarled at Russell and scampered back into the darkness, but Russell knew the boy was alone and had no safe place to be.

It was Russell's duty, then to find a place for people who needed it, a safe, clean place to come for food and education. It was his job to alert the rich to the plight of the poor and convince them it was their moral responsibility to help, that lifting others lifts all. The boy beneath the house had been Bruce Charles, and with daily determination, Russell had befriended the boy and tried to teach him about civility.

Russell looked up at the ceiling. He could see a fat black spider in the corner, working frantically to build a web with its gossamer strands of silk. "I need just two things at first," he said to himself, to the spider, to God. "A small building to start with, to use as a haven for those who need it, and a writer who will take my simple words and make them into a story that will grip this city by the heart."

The spider paused, as if considering the statement, and then returned to its spinning in the dark, dusty corner.

4

Progress Continues in the Raising of the City; Two Workmen Injured

The effort which began in our fair city in 1856 continues, that of raising municipal and other buildings above the mud and resurfacing the ground with stone and packed earth. As any citizen of Chicago knows, one of the major problems here is mud. Due to this concern and with thanks to those gentlemen with foresight and an understanding of construction and engineering, quite a few buildings have already been hoisted up off the soggy land by means of crank-operated jackscrews and set on stilts when they have reached the desired height. While a good number of those buildings have not yet been filled in underneath, sometimes making wind a greater trouble than usual as it blows through the stilts and out to pedestrians on the streets, progress continues, and it has been projected that completion of the raising project may come as soon as two years from now.

Monday morning, while hoisting West's Print Shop and Apothecary, two workmen caught their hands in the jackscrew, which crushed the fingers of one and amputated the hand of the other. The crew's overseer explained that the men had been drinking the night before and had been unduly thoughtless in their work. The man who lost his hand, Herman Strinstein, told this reporter that he was not a drunk and had been careful, but the overseer had been rushing to get the job done so they could move on to the next building by the end of the week.

"I gave my hand for this," Strinstein complained from his bed at Central Hospital. "For the great wooden city, like a slave in Egypt. Now how shall I feed my family? I should like to go home to Germany if I had the means."

George Rainey, Chicago Tribune
June 4, 1871

When Katina went outside to the alley late Sunday morning, the rain had slowed to a drizzle. The air was thick with the small of worms and dead mice. She pulled the brim of her cap down to keep it from blowing away and thought, *I wish never to feel another raindrop. How much water can one city tolerate? We've got a whole lake. That should be plenty.* A passing wagon full of potatoes splashed the bottoms of her trousers but she just shifted the satchel she clutched from one hand to the other and began walking. She was on her way to Michigan Avenue. She had a letter to deliver.

It didn't take long to leave the shanties, saloons, and dance halls behind. The business section of the city was only three blocks to the north, and here was another world, an elegant world. Roads were wide, paved with pine blocks or cobblestones to help alleviate the problem of winter mud and summer dust. Trees, covered with the thick, green leaves of June, lined the streets. Gaslights on wrought iron posts stood on corners and at intervals along the street. Fire hydrants were new and made of cast iron, unlike the wooden, churn-like ones in the slum. Horsecars traveled along steel tracks in the road surfaces. Carriages and tea carts clattered up and down the streets, carrying well-dressed occupants on their way to church. Women, strolling with their husbands, wore gowns trimmed in satin or velvet with proper bustles in the back. The men wore black waistcoats and long jackets with gloves, hats, and carried walking canes.

Although Chicago was a city built primarily of fine Illinois and Wisconsin timber, some of the buildings in the business district were painted to look like marble or stone. Signs on doors and awnings made it clear that establishments' clientele were of the upper class. "Suits for the Discriminating Gentleman," "Alice Morrison's Ladies' Boutique" "Arthur and Addamson, Attorneys at Law." Very different from "The Stick Saloon" on Quincy and "Raymond Atlinger, Ragseller" in Rat's Alley. Even the birds that circled the air around the Steward Grand Theatre and peck the front steps of Crosby's Opera House seemed haughtier than slum birds. A pair of them squawked at Katina from a light pole as she paused to pick a rock from her shoe. She threw the rock at them and they flew away.

Inside Katina's satchel were the only pieces of women's clothing she owned, a white blouse and blue skirt with white piping on the hem, the ones she'd worn when she'd escaped from Willowbrook. She had grown over an inch taller since arriving in Chicago and had to buy a rag from Raymond Atlinger to sew around the hem to bring it back to a decent length.

As was true for many streets in the city, there were wide, wooden sidewalks on both sides of these avenues, in some places three to five off the ground. This way, pedestrians could move more easily from business to business, away from the traffic and mud in the roadway. Katina strolled along the sidewalk, peering into shop windows as she passed. She saw her reflection in beveled-edge window glass and it was a sad sight, indeed. No longer pretty and trusting, she was now scraggly and steely-eyed.

But I remember how to be polite, she thought as she moved from the window. *If I get to talk to them, I'll make up for my appearance with actions. Mother used to say, "Pretty is as pretty does."*

Soon she saw a slice of Lake Michigan through the buildings, and it was only minutes before she found herself on a cobblestoned residential street lined with refined houses face in brick or wooden shingles. Large yards were filled with azaleas and rose of Sharon, and wide flower beds had been newly planted with summer blooms. Front porches were furnished with wicker chairs and potted evergreens. The lake shimmered, its small waves rising and falling like the heartbeat of a gentle giant. Sailboats, steamboats, and barges rode the water, carrying goods from the city to destinations far away.

The Monroe house was three stories tall, built of stone and surrounded by a matching stone wall. Standing on tiptoe, Katina could peer over the wall at the well-tended lawn. There was a whitewashed gazebo, a fishpond, and a cobblestone path through a geometric planting of boxwoods. An air of prosperity hung about the property.

I belong here, Katina thought. *They are family, and I am well-bred and educated. I'll make them understand one day!*

Behind a thick holly bush that hugged the exterior of the stone wall, Katina pulled her skirt on over her trousers then shoved the trousers into the satchel. She exchanged her cap for a scarf she'd bought several months ago and wrapped her short, damp hair as fashionably as she could without a mirror. She was sure she looked like a washerwoman, but at least she looked like a woman.

"Perhaps today is the day," she whispered, taking the note from the satchel. She lifted her head, straightened her shoulders, and walked around the wall to the front gate.

Every other Sunday, Katina visited this house by the lake. After the first, frustrating weeks, during which she believed the family would soon recognize her and take her in, and after calling to them from behind the gate, clutching the bars and pleading, she realized that her persistence and dignity would have to overcome their fear and stubbornness. If she slept outside their house or continued to shout at them, they would have the authorities cart her off to an insane asylum. If she climbed over the wall to confront them, they would have the authorities cart her off to jail. And so, she calmly brought a note to the house every other Sunday, dressed as best she could on the chance she might come face to face with one of the family members.

She pulled the chain of the brass bell at the top of the gate and waited.

As fresh raindrops fell and dampened her scarf, she stood and watched for a face to peek out from between a pair of downstairs curtains or through the ribs of upstairs blinds. Often she would catch a glimpse of the Monroe family. There was a father, thin and light-haired, and a mother, pudgy with dark hair. There was a daughter a little younger than Katina, with hair piled on her hair and adorned in ribbons. Who was this girl to Katina? A second cousin? Perhaps even a niece? Why had Katina never heard of the Monroes in Chicago back when she lived in Georgia. She had wondered this often.

The family in the stone house would sometimes glance out after she rang the bell at the gate, and then shake their heads and draw back into the shadows of their home. No one would come out to meet Katina, but they knew she was there. And they had her notes, the ones that that repeated the same information over and over again, notes that maybe, someday, would make them realize who it was that stood beyond the gate.

Today, the maid came out to the porch and the sound of the bell and clapped her hands. "Leave us alone, you!"

Across the distance of the yard, Katina looked the maid in the eye. Perhaps the maid never gave the notes to the family at all. Perhaps she threw them all away and the family never read them. But there was nothing else to do but to keep trying. Katina had made a life for herself in Rat's Alley, but if she thought it would never get any better, she knew she would go mad.

"On, now!" shouted the maid. "Or I'll send out the dog!"

The dog. Katina had seen it tied to the porch on occasion. It was quite a barker. She guessed it could also be quite a biter.

Katina held up the newest note and slipped it through the bars of the gate. It fluttered to the walkway and landed in a puddle.

"Now!" said the maid.

Katina turned away and returned to the holly bush where she gritted her teeth against the familiar sting of disappointment. Then she pulled out her trousers and became William once more.

The walk back to her boardinghouse always felt much longer than the walk to Michigan Avenue. As the lake disappeared behind her amid the tall buildings, she felt as if she were being swallowed alive, sucked back into a great monster whose belly was Rat's Alley. The bustle in the streets—the arguments of men beside an overturned fish car, the laughter of children in a churchyard, the braying of an impatient mule, the clanging of the courthouse fire bell telling the city that something, somewhere, was burning—all these sounds tangled in her ears. The satchel grew heavy and she had to force one foot in front of the other.

On the sagging stoop outside the entrance to the Stick Saloon on Quincy Street, Alice Montague and Becky Alaimo sat with parasols over their heads, looking glum. Their frilly red dresses seemed wilted.

"Mornin', William," Becky said as Katina passed. "You're a wet, dreadful sight."

"I could offer the same compliment," said Katina. "Why are you sitting outside?"

"Oh," said Alice, "Madame Jocelyn is in a snit. She is actin' crazy, throwin' chairs and cussin'. There is hardly a customer now, so we thought it best to be out of the way 'til she was done."

"Does she get in a snit often?" asked Katina.

Alice nodded. "I think she's gettin' meaner with old age. But what can we do? Can't quit. I ain't never worked nowhere but a saloon before and I need to make a livin'."

"Yes," said Becky. "She pays up and so we put up with it."

There was a sudden scream from the end of the street. Katina glanced up and saw a woman on the corner, flailing her arms and yelling at the top of her lungs. A man was trying to grab her. Katina squinted and recognized the woman as her landlady, Meg Brandermill. And there was a lot of blood on the front of her dress.

"Mrs. Brandermill!" Katina shouted. She left Alice and Becky and ran up the street, trying not to trip in the ruts and mud. When she reached the corner, she slammed the heel of her hands against the man's back, sending him to the ground with a grunt. "Leave her alone!" Katina said. "Get away from her!"

"God help me!" cried Mrs. Brandermill, her hands holding her face. Her fingers were streaked in red.

The man rolled over and scrambled to his feet, and as he did, Katina turned with her safety stick in her hand. "Don't touch her!"

It was then she recognized Russell Cosgrove. He didn't look as composed as he had the night before, with his hair knocked in all directions and his hands held up as if he thought she would, indeed, hit him. "Wait!" he said, panting. "I was only trying to help!"

Katina's mouth fell open in confusion.

"Ohh!" moaned Mrs. Brandermill, leaning over and holding her knees. "Oh, why? God have mercy on me!"

"I'm trying to help, William," said Russell. "Now help me help her or get out of the way!"

"All right," said Katina, her voice stripped of its fury. She pocketed her safety stick, turned to Mrs. Brandermill, and both she and Russell held out their hands to try to steady the woman. The woman seemed mad with pain. "Mrs. Brandermill, it's William," said Katina. "Please let us take you home. You're terribly hurt."

"I can't go home!" Mrs. Brandermill wept, her head hanging down and her words coming in great whoops. Katina could see the blood on the side of her bonnet and a great gash in Mrs. Brandermill's cheek.

"What happened, ma'am, please tell," said Russell.

"Men wouldn't understand. It's a woman's plight!"

"Oh, we would," insisted Katina. "We can take you to a doctor, if you'd rather. Just tell us what's wrong so we can assist you."

"I haven't money for a doctor!"

"That doesn't matter," said Russell. He stooped down close to the woman's face. "Please. Let us take you. We can worry about payment later."

"No! Oh, you just....you...." said Mrs. Brandermill. Then she gasped and fainted, dropped to the roadside.

"Help me," said Russell, giving Katina a quick glance. "I haven't got money for a doctor but St. Andrew's Church is close, and a house of God will certainly help us find a charitable physician. But we must be quick!"

Katina took Mrs. Brandermill's arms and Russell took her ankles and lifted her, barely, off the street. The woman was small but her pregnancy had given her extra weight that Katina knew was too much for her to hold for very long. But then, standing beside them, were Becky and Alice, their hands to their mouths and their eyes huge. "Will she die?" asked Alice.

"We'll do all we can to keep her from it," said Russell.

The four of them carried Mrs. Brandermill a full two and a half blocks to the door of St. Andrew's Church, up the wooden steps and into the dark, candle-lit sanctuary.

They laid the woman gently in the aisle, and while Becky and Alice knelt beside her and patted her hand, Katina and Russell ran in search of the pastor.

"Hello? Someone, quickly!" called Katina. "We have an injured woman. Please!" Her voice echoed in the deep recesses of the church. She'd not been inside a church since leaving the orphan asylum, and being in one now made her uncomfortable, as if God wouldn't remember who she was.

"Hello?" shouted Russell. "Pastor Botkins?"

Katina tried a door to one side of the altar, but it was locked. Russell went to the second one and reached for the knob. Just then, a portly, bald man in black garb came out. He was frowning and wiping crumbs from his mouth. "What is this commotion in my church?" he demanded. "What are you all about here?"

Russell took the man firmly by the elbow and turned him so he could see down the aisle. "We've a hurt woman in need of immediate attention. Have you knowledge of a charitable physician who could attend her, and quickly?"

Pastor Botkins made a grunting noise and rolled his eyes. "Another one," he mumbled.

"Another one what?" asked Katina.

"Another one losing a baby, can't you see? The blood, the way she's cramped up? Let her lose it. God knows we've enough living in this slum as it is. The mother won't die. They hardly ever do."

Russell grabbed the man's shoulders and shook him. "*God* knows? God knows no such thing! How dare you say such a thing!"

"And it's more than losing a baby," said Katina. "She's been beaten, and badly!"

"Get her out of my sanctuary," said Pastor Botkins. He

jerked from Russell's grasp and shook a threatening finger at the man. "Now, before I have you thrown out. All that bloody mess is spoiling the runner on the floor."

Russell gave an exasperated cry and threw up his hands. "Your sanctuary? You pious pig! God forgive you and your deadly arrogance! William, let's go elsewhere!"

On the runner in the aisle, Mrs. Brandermill had begun to writhe in pain, her feet kicking at the floor and her teeth gnashing the air. Her dress was now completely drenched in blood.

"Oh," said Alice, no longer trying to comfort the woman but flat back against a pew. "She gonna die, I can smell it!"

"No!" said Russell. "We can't let her die, we—"

But Becky said, "She gonna die, sir. She got but a second and if we move her, her last moment on Earth will be nothin' but jostlin' on top of the pain."

Katina looked toward the altar. Pastor Botkins had vanished, most likely to finish his lunch. She looked back at Mrs. Brandermill. "Who beat you, Meg? Was it John?"

"Don't matter now," said Alice, shaking her head. "Knowing who beat her won't keep her from dying."

"But it does matter!" insisted Katina.

Slowly, Mrs. Brandermill nodded.

"So, it was John?" pressed Katina. Mrs. Brandermill nodded again.

"I said it don't matter," said Alice. "Leave her be."

The four stared at the woman on the floor. Then Becky said, "Rest her soul. She's gone."

And Mrs. Brandermill was, indeed, gone. With a quiet sigh, her head rolled over to rest on Pastor Botkin's runner. Her shoes stopped digging at the floor. Her eyes, half open, no longer blinked. The sweet landlady was dead.

5

"Sweet Jesus," whispered Becky. "She's gone."

Alice crossed herself and kissed her knuckle.

Russell lifted the dead woman and held her, saying through clenched teeth, "This should not happen."

Katina stared, not believing her kind young landlady was no longer alive, nor was the baby she had so desired. Mr. Brandermill should be arrested. He should face judgment with jury and judge. He should be imprisoned! But Katina's mouth was so dry she couldn't speak. Furious tears welled in her eyes but she dug them away.

The four stayed there for what seemed like a very long time before they at last lifted Meg Brandermill and carried her to the undertaker's shop on Jackson Street. The undertaker, a scarecrowish man covered in sawdust from the coffins he built, brushed his hands off and demanded to know who would pay for the burial. "I don't work for folks who don't pay. I got to make a living, even if I make it off the dead."

"I'll get the money to you in the morning," said Russell without hesitation. Then the undertaker scribbled a bill for a coffin and burial at the paupers' plot near the South Branch of the river. He handed it to Russell.

Becky and Alice left for the Stick Saloon, leaving Russell and Katina outside the undertaker's shop in the drizzling rain, silent with their own thoughts. As the late Sunday afternoon traffic of carts, wagons, mules and pedestrians worked its way here and there with the usual clamor, neither Russell nor Katina could move.

Katina's only female friend was dead. Meg would never again peer through the door and ask about the plays, would never again offer to help with pinning laundry to the wires behind the tenement. Katina crossed her arms, bowed her head, and cried silently. At last she spoke through parched lips. "Where are you going to get money for the burial?"

"I have a little," said Russell.

"It was her husband who beat her to death."

"Oh, God. Have they other children?"

"No, the baby would have been their first."

"I'm glad there will be no little ones left behind with a parent who is so brutal. Or alone when the parent is locked up and away."

"Yes," said Katina. "The man's a brute. I loved Mrs. Brandermill. The man's an animal and never deserved her."

"There has to be a way," said Russell, lifting his gaze to the sky as if there might be a message set in the clouds. Katina watched him and found herself once more attracted to his rugged face, his strong voice, and his air of compassion for others. His canvas coat and the front of his white shirt were smeared with blood but it didn't seem to offend him. "There must be a way," he repeated.

"A way for what?"

Russell looked back at Katina, and she was startled with the crystal clarity of his blue eyes. "A way to change circumstances. To make a difference. William, I need help."

"Help for what? To alert the authorities about Mr. Brandermill?"

"You'll do that, yes. But I mean help for a greater task."

Katina didn't have the energy to ask him what he meant. She was suddenly dizzy, exhausted. Stars swam in her vision. But she couldn't let herself pass out. She wouldn't. She'd seen worse than this in her life and she was still standing.

"Listen," said Russell, putting his hand on her shoulder. It made her feel better; it made her feel safer. She wished he would keep it there for a long time. "I haven't had a midday meal. Would you care to join me? Alert a constable about Mr. Brandermill. Take as long as you need. His poor wife deserved to have the truth known. Then come to Sallee's Butcher Shop on Fifth and go up the steps on the side. My apartment is at the top."

Katina stammered, "Well....well, I—"

"Have you got better plans for dinner?" asked Russell. Then he smiled a small smile, and Katina knew that he knew that she had nowhere to go for a good meal. He was teasing because he could see she was as scrawny as any person in this area of Chicago, and he knew that free food was always welcome.

"I'd be happy to come," she said. "I have some bread in my flat I can bring."

"No," said Russell. He reached out and tousled her hat, nearly knocking it off, and she was instantly chagrined. For a moment she'd forgotten she was charading as a boy and imagined he'd seen her as Katina, not William. "Bring nothing, lad. And the next time, you will cook for me."

"All right," said Katina. "I won't be long."

Although the city of Chicago was well-supplied with fire-alarm boxes which citizens could use to alert the courthouse in the event of a fire, there was no such system for alerting the police department of crimes. Katina had to walk for twenty-five minutes before she found a constable. She described the beating death of Mrs. Brandermill at the hands of her husband. Although the policeman agreed to talk to Mr. Brandermill, Katina could tell he didn't feel the same urgency she did.

"Thank you," he said simply. "I'll look into it."

"You will arrest him?"

"I need to talk with him and any witnesses to see if I should arrest him."

"Need to arrest him? Listen to me! He did it! His wife confirmed that as she lay dying, but he will surely lie to you."

"That is for us to determine," he said, his mustache twitching.

"Are you bribed, too?" Katina cried. "Are you going to ignore it because the criminals have paid you to leave well enough alone?"

The constable grabbed her arm. "Don't you speak to me like that, boy. I'll haul you in for anything I like, don't think I won't. Now, get out of my way. I'll speak to Mr. Brandermill and hear his side of the story."

"Make sure you go to the undertaker's shop on Jackson Street and see Mrs. Brandermill's side of the story!"

Her body shaking with frustration and rage, Katina walked to Sallee's Butcher Shop. She knew this store, and had even purchased some scrap meat here. It was on the same block of Fifth Avenue as the theater, only six buildings up. Katina wondered if Russell had ever been in the audience. Was he even aware of the theater? Or worse, did he know the theater was there but considered drama to be trivial and a waste of time?

Good heavens, she scolded herself as she climbed the steps. *What difference can it make? This man can never be more than a casual acquaintance. What does it matter what he thinks of plays or theater?*

There were two rooms, the front room a combined kitchen and sitting area, and the second, visible through an open door, a tiny bedroom. The furniture was no better than Katina's own, scratched and mismatched. Two chairs had been pulled up to a small wooden table in the front room. There were no windows here, but the room was brightened, surprisingly, by two dark yellow roses and a cluster of purple violets in a small pottery vase. Something was at a rolling boil in a pot on the cookstove and Russell was digging at the contents with a spoon.

"Hello," he said, stirring furiously. The front of his hair had curled up with the steam. "I thought I would make a soup. But I'm afraid it's out of control. Most of the water is cooked away and I've no more water in the bucket. The vegetables are starting to stick to the pan. This is foul."

Katina's heart began to beat faster as she realized she was alone with Russell in his apartment. "It doesn't smell bad."

"Smell can be deceiving."

Katina took off her coat and began to remove her hat but stopped. Not that a hat held the secret to her identity, but it helped. She'd have to show bad manners and keep it on. She hoped Russell didn't ask about it.

"Curses," said Russell as he pulled the pan from the flame. "Look at this. A mushy disaster." He lifted the spoon. The potatoes and beans had cooked down into something reminiscent of pig slop. "What do you think? Food fit for two bachelors?"

"Of course," said Katina. "I've had worse."

Russell plopped scoopfuls of the once-soup into two bowls,

handed one to Katina, and sat down across for her at the table with the other bowl. "Oh, but you haven't tasted it yet."

"We can call it scorched stew rather than soup," offered Katina with a small chuckle. She lifted the spoon and dipped it into the steaming mess in the bowl. Before she could lift the spoon to her lips, Russell was saying, "Lord, bless this food, such as it is, to the nourishment of our bodies and the strength of our hearts. Take Mrs. Brandermill into your arms forever. Amen."

"Amen," echoed Katina. Then she glanced up at him. He was looking at her with his intense blue eyes. He smiled, and she managed a smile back. Then he took a bite, grimaced, and wheezed. "Not bad," he coughed.

Katina made a face then tasted a mouthful. It was all she could do to swallow. The flavor was that of ash, tin, and scalded beans. She knew how to cook. It was one of the skills she'd learned in her past life. But she couldn't admit that to Russell. She took another bite and told herself at least it was food and it was free.

"Fond of that hat?" asked Russell around another mouthful of the stew.

"Oh." Katina touched the brim and shrugged. "It's a gift from...my brother." *My brother? Now you're going to lie out loud to him? Be quiet, don't go making up things or it'll only be worse.*

"I've family in the city, too," said Russell, tipping his head toward the vase with the roses and violets. "Those are from my mother's garden. My parents live across the South Branch of the river, on De Koven Street. My mother always had a beautiful but tiny flower garden, always in bloom a week at least before her neighbors. I visit my parents once a week."

"I see."

"So, are you employed, William Monroe?"

"Yes, at Anderson's Market. But also—" she slowed her breathing so she wouldn't sound uneasy in revealing her true passion—"I'm a writer for the MacPherson Theater, on this very street. An actor also, but mainly a writer. It's what I love to do the most."

"A writer?" Russell sat straight.

"Yes," said Katina. "Of plays. Someday I will create a brilliant drama that will be talked about everywhere. I will be rich and famous."

Russell was silent for a moment, his gaze going to the far wall.

What is he thinking?

Katina interrupted the silence. "Enough about me. How long have you lived in this flat?"

"Nearly a month." Russell looked back at her and wiped his mouth on his sleeve, something Katina was sure he couldn't have done had he known he was in a lady's company. "You say you are a writer?"

Katina nodded. "Coming here was your choice?"

"Yes. I felt drawn here, or sent, I'm not sure which. I have work to do."

"What kind of work?"

Russell stirred his spoon in the stew. Then he said, "Do you believe things can happen for a reason? Yes, there is a reason for everything that happens, but that sometimes, we're brought into situations for a purpose?"

"I'm not sure what you mean."

"You and me meeting last night, for example," Russell said. "A chance meeting, one might think, but think again. There could be destiny involved."

"You mean fate, like a seer's or sage's prediction?"

"No, I mean true destiny. That if we live life with our eyes open, we'll come upon things that are supposed to be there for us, things to help us continue."

Katina looked for a napkin with which to wipe her mouth but Russell had put none out, so she used her sleeve, as well. "I guess I never thought about it."

Russell's expression shifted to one of hesitant excitement and this made his face look like that of a little boy. "Listen," he said. "I haven't told anybody this yet, but I moved here, having quit college, because I felt called to do something about the terrible conditions of the people here."

"Who do you think you are," Katina asked, laughing unintentionally in disbelief, "some kind of preacher or miracle worker?"

"Between you and me, I don't know what I am."

"Do you earn a wage somewhere?"

"Not at the moment. I've been busy trying to determine how to go about my task, getting to know the people, the establishments. Trying to convince the *Tribune* to publish an article. I've been trying alone and making little progress. Until today. When you came to the defense of Mrs. Brandermill, I saw something that impressed me. And now, I discover you are a writer."

"What does being a writer have to do with anything?"

"My own words are clumsy. I thought I had a skill I don't really have. I need a story in the *Tribune* about the plight of our neighbors. There are many poor in Chicago, but many rich as well. I want the wealthy to stop for a moment and look at the poor, to see their humanity, to see how much they could help if they only would. I've tried to talk to reporters with no luck. But if I had someone who could take my words and make them speak with clarity and force, then—"

"Wait a moment," said Katina. Her heart skipped a beat. She had a fleeting image of Russell sitting close beside her, reading her writings, touching her arm in appreciation. Of them spending time together, sharing meals, being close. "I have a job," she said, shaking the images from her head. "I have enough trouble taking care of myself. I might defend a friend—which clearly did no good—and I might write plays, but I'm not up to whatever your grand vision might be."

"William, you may be young, but you are feisty. And kindhearted. I need a writer, playwright or otherwise. And I need something who will help me secure a building and create a safe haven for those like Mrs. Brandermill and Bruce Charles. If we don't help, who will?"

"You can't save the world."

"I can do what I can do."

"But you have no true sense of who I am."

"I sense you are someone good."

Katina looked at the floor. She suddenly smelled fire, and heard the crackling of flames. But it was not the burned meal nor Russell's cookstove behind her. It was an old fire, burning in her memory, mocking her inability to help her mother and sisters. They were dying in a flame as she sat helplessly in a tree. Doing nothing. Watching and doing nothing.

You did nothing.

"You've made a mistake. I can't help anybody." Her words sounded flat and hard, and she didn't care.

Russell turned his palms up in resignation. "All right. I'm making presumptions and demands. Do you forgive me?"

Katina nodded and looked back in her bowl. The food had cooled now and a skin had formed on the top.

"Would you like to talk about baseball?" Russell asked, trying to be cheerful. "I'm fascinated with the Chicago White Stockings. I think all young men would dream of wielding a bat and watching the ball fly. And such a salary they earn! As much as $2,500 a year. Do you think you'd like to be a baseball player when you're grown?"

When I'm grown, Katina thought glumly as Russell continued talking. *I* am *grown up. I'm your age nearly, yet you see a child sitting here. And a boy child at that. Will I ever be able to tell you the truth?*

And if I do, what will you think of me then?

And will you ever feel your pulse race when you are near me, as I feel mine when I am near you?

6

Monday morning, Russell awoke knowing he needed to find a job. William's questions about his work and income had left him uneasy all night. He realized that it was wrong to live on the money he'd saved from not attending college, as that money would need to go to managing the safe haven once it was established. And so, as soon as the mercantile across the street opened, he spent fifty cents on a wood box full of polish, rags, and a brush, and said to himself, "I'll be a bootblack." It was an unusual jog for a young man—usually children or old men polished shoes—but the work was portable, and he could do it as often as time allowed.

With the polish box beneath his arm, he stopped at the undertaker's and gave the man three dollars for Mrs. Brandermill's coffin and burial. Then he went out to find some customers in the business district. He would work all morning and then go to the *Tribune* to try again to entice a reporter to his cause.

Bruce Charles spied him from the doorway of an empty tobacco shop, jumped into the street, and grabbed the tail of Russell's coat. "Can I come?" the boy asked after Russell explained his mission. "There are pockets to pick there, and I promise I won't hit nobody with a pipe."

"I'm not going to pick pockets," Russell explained. "I'm going to make an honest penny. And if you'd like to learn a trade and that has nothing to do with pockets, you are welcome to join me."

Bruce grinned. "Yes!"

But the gentlemen with the muddy shoes and boots treading the wide, raised walkways of State Street weren't easily impressed, and it was clear they thought a young man in a wrinkled coat and a young boy with no shoes at all were up to no good. As Russell stood on the street next to the door of Mrs. Abigail Archer's Fine French Millinery, offering shines as politely as possible, the pedestrians up on the wooden walk picked up their paces in order to pass by.

After a half hour, Bruce smacked Russell in the arm and said, "You ain't doin' it right. Ain't you never sold nothin' before?"

"No. And neither have you."

"Let me have a go," said Bruce. As a tall man in a top hat passed by, Bruce shouted, "Hello! You there, sir! You look like a pile of walking cow dung with them messy boots! Lemme give you a polish."

Russell jerked Bruce back by his collar.

"What's the matter?" asked Bruce. "He did look dreadful, his coat all pressed and his boots all messed."

"Have you never heard the term, 'You can catch more flies with honey than with vinegar?' Who would stop for a boy who just insulted them?"

"I insulted him?"

"We need another strategy."

And so, they found a spot at the end of one raised sidewalk in the shade of a tall maple tree. Standing here, they were level with the pedestrians and weren't calling up to them. It seemed less aggressive. Russell instructed Bruce to be quiet while Russell spoke to the men who passed. "A moment, sir, to shine your shoes?"

This worked. The men on the sidewalk seemed less threatened by someone not at eye level with them, and by noon Bruce and Russell had run out of polish and had made a dollar and five cents. They were coated with the mud thrown up by passing horses and carriages but Russell was satisfied. He gave Bruce thirty cents, at which the boy grumbled that if he'd been allowed to pick a few pockets he'd have come away with more, and sent the boy off. Russell stuck the polish box back under his arm and walked to the Tribune Building at the corner of Dearborn and Madison.

But this day was much like Saturday. Although Russell spent a good five minutes scraping the last of the mud from his clothes and the last of the polish onto his own shoes before entering the four-story building with its arched windows and doorway, he was given no more than curious and then irritated glances by reporters and businessmen inside. He placed the polish box beneath a bench by the wall then asked the receptionist if there was not one reporter with whom he could speak. But she turned up her nose, hopped from her chair, and padded down the long hall, the bustle of her skirt bouncing. A moment later she was back with two men with trim mustaches who told Russell he was a nuisance and not welcome to return.

"I only need a minute," said Russell. "This is important."

"We haven't got minute, sir. Please leave."

Russell turned to look each man, in turn, directly in the eye. "How do you know you haven't got time for me? We haven't spoken."

"And we won't!" said one man. "You'll have the bottom of our shoes in your back if you do not leave. Now."

The men took his arms, but Russell jerked free, spun on his heel, and held out his shaking fist. "This whole office be damned! You and your pomposity!" He snatched the polish box from beneath the bench and stormed out the door.

Back on the sunny street, he stared up at the building, his face flushed with fury. *How dare they?* he thought. *Why won't they even listen?*

"It's not working," he said aloud as he walked back to the butcher shop. His unbuttoned canvas coat flapped out behind him like the wings of a giant bird. He didn't care if people he passed heard him talking to himself and thought him soft in the head. "Why isn't it working?" His boots pounded the ground in rhythm. "But I can't get discouraged. There are other newspapers. Yet the *Tribune* is the most wildly read and would have been the best forum." He walked on, his thoughts racing. "Maybe I'm going at this wrong. Perhaps I should find a building first, approach the owner with the money I have left as a deposit, then open the safe haven, even if I can only afford to run it for a week. Perhaps a reporter would then realize there was a story and would come visit and write it up. That must be the answer. I wasn't drawn here to have this dream die."

It was when he reached the base of the steps to his flat that he remembered the MacPherson Theater. William had mentioned it. But he knew the building was not vacant; it was a theater, a business.

"But," he said to himself, "I would guess it's not used most of the time. The actors have jobs during the day, like William. And there wouldn't be a performance every night." He felt his heart leap at the possibility.

He put the polish box under the bottom step then walked down to the theater and stood starting at the old stable from the middle of the road as riders and wagon drivers swerved around him. The low roofed building was about thirty feet wide along the road, extending back at least fifty feet; its shingles looked in decent repair. Next door was Skinner's Pawn Shop. Russell rattled the theater door, trying to force open a crack that was big enough to see through, but the lock held tightly.

"What are you doing there? This is my building."

There was a dark-haired, lanky young man beside him, shading his face and frowning.

Russell held out his hand but the other man would not take it. "I'm Russell Cosgrove. I meant no harm. I only wanted to see inside."

"Why? Has your horse gotten away from you and crawled in through the locked door, so you must go after him?"

Russell laughed then saw it was the wrong thing to do. The man wasn't smiling. "No, sir. Last evening, I was talking with a member of your acting troupe, and I was curious as to the layout of the building."

"Are you an actor?"

"No."

"Why, then? With whom did you speak?"

"William Monroe. I'm looking for a building to use during daylight hours and occasional evenings. A place that has space and is well-built. And won't require much rent."

"And William Monroe told you this place is available during the day for little rent?"

"No. But I thought there was no harm in looking."

The other man crossed his arms, one brow up, waiting for Russell to explain.

"I have plans," Russell said, hesitating then barging ahead.

"I'm going to raise contributions and open a safe haven for some of our neighborhood's poorest. I need a place where folks can have a meal, find warmth in the winter and a cool drink in the summer, where children who find themselves on the streets can learn to read and write and where—"

The man shook his head. "You're talking lunacy. There's never been such a thing."

"There should be."

The man stared at Russell then looked down. But his face seemed to be softening. "Who are you, a preacher?"

"I'm a bootblack, looking to help my neighbors."

"But this place is a theater."

"I know. Could I take a look inside?"

"I'm busy today. I'm picking up a fresh supply of nails for fences we're repairing at Thichnor's varnish shop. I was on my way to the hardware when I saw you."

"One quick look? Please?"

"You say you know William?"

"We shared a meal last night. May I look?"

The man let out a deep, agitated breath. "All right, but only for a moment." He unlocked the door and it swung wide.

It was cool and dark inside, and the shadows Russell first took for sleeping bodies along the floor were actually rows of benches facing the back of the wide room. The smell was one of old hay, dirt, and kerosene. As his eyes adjusted, he could see the stage at the other end of the room and several lanterns on hooks along the walls beside small, latched windows. It was indeed a theater. And it was indeed a good-sized room, a place that could be a temporary safe haven until someone with wealth was willing to help purchase another, larger place.

"Do you see, Mr. Cosgrove?" asked the man. "I don't believe this would suit your needs."

Russell walked toward the stage, trying to imagine how many people could eat here, where a table might be set up for tutoring. He pulled the curtain aside along the rope tie and stepped onto the stage.

The next instant he heard a scream that froze his blood and stopped him in his tracks.

7

She hadn't meant to scream.

Now they'll find me for sure!

She put her hand over her mouth, knowing it was futile but not knowing anything else to do. She had already screamed.

Go away go away go away!

One man shouted, "Who is that?"

The voice sounded familiar. She took a breath and held it. On the heels of the first shout came, "Hello! Who is there?"

Katina, her face tucked inside the collar of her coat and sitting in the far back corner of the old tack stall, slowly pulled the collar down far enough to see out. There were two figures outside the stall now, staring in. She knew they could see her in the shadows, and she had no defense. Even her safety stick was somewhere on Quincy Street, dropped and lost when she'd come to Mrs. Brandermill's defense.

There was a second of silence, with only the sound of fluttering swallow wings in the rafters.

Then the first man's voice again. "Hello?"

"Adam?" Katina said softly.

"William?"

"Adam, it's me. If you have gun, for heaven's sake, don't shoot."

"William?" said the other man. Katina knew this voice, too. She tucked her face back inside her coat, thinking, *I'm safe, thank the Lord. But why is it him? Why did he have to find me like this?*

The second voice belonged to Russell Cosgrove.

"What on God's green earth are you doing here?" asked Adam. A hand moved forward, touched her shoulder, and she pulled her face out of her collar again. Adam and Russell were kneeling now, looking at her as if she'd grown a second nose.

Adam was squinting with his bad eyes.

"Are you hurt?" he asked.

"No. Not yet."

"Not yet?" asked Russell.

Katina signed painfully and said, "I should have left it alone. I shouldn't have opened my big mouth. I should have said nothing to the constable. I'm in deep trouble." She got up slowly, wriggling her toes inside her shoes to rid them of a tingling sensation. She nodded at the brocade satchel on the floor beside her.

"Everything I own," she said, "is in there. And I've no place to live."

"Did your building burn down?" asked Adam.

"No, but it might as well have." She looked directly in his eyes and saw a concern there that almost made her cry. Almost. She would not cry in front of this man. "Mr. Brandermill was questioned by the authorities at my request, as you know. The authorities described to him the person who alerted them. In other words, they described me to Mr. Brandermill. Of course, John Brandermill would be one of those who, like many other criminals in our neighborhood, bribe police with their gambling income to leave them alone. So, the man's still in his tenement, still landlord there, waiting for me to come back so he can—" Katina couldn't say more. She could only imagine what might come after that. All she knew was that she had to hide.

Russell put his arm around her shoulder. He smelled good, of cheap soap and tenderness. "William, I'm so sorry. This is dreadful!"

Adam said, "I don't understand."

The three of them went to the front of the theater and sat on a bench. Katina related the story of Meg Brandermill's death. Both men agreed that it was dangerous for William now, not only because Mr. Brandermill was a violent man but because none of them knew who his cohorts were, and how could she avoid them if she didn't even know them?

"Are you certain he knows it was you who told?" asked Adam.

"When I returned to the boardinghouse, I saw him looking

out his window at me. I could tell by his expression that something foul was brewing in his mind."

"Then you need a place to hide," said Adam.

Katina groaned, exasperated. "Why do you think I sneaked in here, genius? Because I prefer hard floors with scratchy straw crumbs to a bed?"

"William, for all your good intentions, why did you say anything?" asked Adam. "Mrs. Brandermill died and nothing, not even the arrest of her husband, will bring her back. Now my theater must be shut down until he's arrested so you can stay out of sight?"

"I have a better idea," said Russell. "William, why don't you come stay with me?"

Katina looked at Russell. "What?"

"I have space, two chairs an extra blanket, and we can sleep head to toe if you don't mind my socks in your face. And you know what a good cook I am." He winked.

"Oh, well, no," stammered Katina, but she couldn't think of a plausible reason to refuse Russell's offer. She did need a place to stay and a friend was offering it to her. But how could she live in a tiny, two-room apartment with this man and not have him discover who she really was ? How could she live so close to this strong, kind, handsome man and not find herself, well…

Falling in love, she thought. *No! It would be better just to continue to hide her in this old stable until Mr. Brandermill is dealt with.*

And so, she said, "Russell, it's generous of you, but I can't afford to pay and so I can't afford to stay with you. But I'm—"

"Don't be ridiculous," said Russell. "I wouldn't expect you to pay me in money. But I do have an idea, one that will benefit us both."

"What is that?" she asked hesitantly.

"In lieu of cash, you can write for me. You told me yourself you're a writer."

"He's a fine writer," said Adam.

"Write for me, William. I have a desk, ink, paper. My notes are in desperate need of reshaping. You can share my meals, the heat from my stove, until it is safe again for you to come out. All right?"

"But I only write plays."

"A writer can write anything, play or essay. Do you agree?"

"Of course, he does," said Adam. He looked at Katina. "You do agree, don't you?"

"Agreed," Katina heard herself say.

Adam patted Katina's head then hopped up. "I must be gone with my nails. Where do you live, sir? I shall come by later to check on our young friend."

"My flat is at the end of this block above Sallee's Butcher Shop. Just listen and you'll hear the owner shouting. It's hard to miss."

"Done, then," said Adam. He hurried to the door but paused there and called over his shoulder, "William, how did you get into the theater?"

Katina pointed at a loose shutter.

Adam said, "And I thought the place was secure. Blast it all!" And then he was gone.

Katina knew she was shaking—her trembling rattled her to her teeth—but she bit the inside of her cheek to control it. *Writing as payment? Katina, be calm now. This is certainly manageable. Room and board in exchange for an essay or two?* It was more than fair.

And yet…!

Russell had gone back to the stall but now stood before Katina, holding her satchel and smiling his startlingly beautiful smile. "Let's get you settled in," he said. "This will work out well. I do believe this was meant to be. Come, William, you look as if you've swallowed something foul!"

Katina pulled her hat low down over her eyes, shrugged the collar of her coat back up to obscure her chin, and followed Russell down the street to the butcher shop. With only her eyes visible, she observed those who passed them on the street. Mothers, holding babies in tightly wrapped cloaks, headed for the market. Dirty children laughed and chased each other with sticks. A young woman in a plain skirt and shawl, her own age, stood with her beau and mooned over him with starstruck eyes.

None of them seemed to be looking for her. She knew she would be safe, tucked away in Russell's apartment. *But it's all so…intimate, much too intimate. Sharing this table, his washbowl, his blanket.* She muffled a cough brought on by the grit rising from the road.

It was dark inside the apartment, and the air still hinted of the burned meal they'd shared the previous evening. Russell dropped the satchel on the table, went into the tiny bedroom, and pushed the curtains aside. Dim light filled the apartment. He came back into the front room and said, "My journals are on the desk by the bed. You can sort through them to see if you can make sense of the contents while I'm gone. There are pages and pages, but something a writer can hopefully put into a form that is publishable. And make yourself at home. I've a few potatoes in that bin, some cornbread, some boiled eggs, and water in the bucket." He raised one eyebrow and Katina knew he was trying to ease her worries. She wondered how it would feel to have him hold her close, to touch her face and caress her back. How safe would that feel. How wonderful.

Stop thinking like that!

Katina said, "Thank you. I appreciate all of this."

"I've a lot of things to do this afternoon," said Russell. "I've got a potential contributor to visit, the proprietor of the Stick Saloon."

"You don't mean Madame Jocelyn."

"Do you know the woman?"

"I know of her."

"Do you think she'd be willing to make a donation?"

"Ha! You'll only know if you ask."

Russell ran his fingers through his hair. He glanced at Katina with earnest uncertainty. "Do I look all right? Presentable?"

"You look quite handsome," said Katina then she quickly amended, "I mean you look good, presentable." *Watch your words, Katina!*

"Good." Russell opened the door then said, "I apologize if I seemed to take your concerns lightly, William. You are probably more frightened now than at any time of your life."

"Actually, I've been more frightened, believe it or not," said Katina, giving him a tough-boy look.

"I know you feel coerced into helping me, but I appreciate it just the same."

"I'm happy to help."

Then he was gone, the door closing behind him, and she heard his heavy footsteps pounding down to the street. From below, Katina could hear a man and woman yelling at each other, something about maggots in a delivery of pigs' feet.

She sat at the table, looked at the bread on the plate beneath the linen, and then let the linen fall back. She had no appetite. A mouse raced across the floor and she watched it go.

"Happy to help? How can I be happy to help?" she said to herself. "I should be at Anderson's Market. Mr. Anderson is surely angry, wondering what happened to his errand boy. I shall lose that job and when I do return, he'll withhold my last week's earnings as punishment." She slammed her elbows down on the tabletop. "Russell Cosgrove, do you see the result of trying to do good for others? Do you see this refugee, hiding in your home, now without any income? Isn't it best to be concerned about your own welfare? Isn't that enough?"

The shouting downstairs stopped. A customer must have come into the shop.

"Fine," said Katina, looking through the door at the small desk in the corner of the back room. "I'll write your articles, Russell, and when Mr. Brandermill is in jail, I will leave you to your dreams of a safe haven. My debt will be paid."

Katina's gaze found the bright yellow roses and violets in the vase. And she wondered for a brief moment if beautiful things could really exist in a troubled place, and if a dream of hope could bloom in a world filled with despair.

8

Police Captain's Barn, Outbuildings Consumed

South Side Police Captain Fritz Logan returned to his home on Griswold Street after work Wednesday night to find his barn and several outbuildings burning to the ground and his home scorched. The cause appears to have been several boys, including Logan's own son, Geoffrey, smoking cigars in the outhouse. Also damaged were the fruit trees in the yard, an animal pen in the neighboring yard of Mr. and Mrs. Francis LaVin, and a thirty-five-foot stretch of wooden sidewalk along the road.

Firemen quickly responded with their steam engine, the "Little Colonel." The flames were extinguished within the hour thanks to the quick actions of the men, though Captain Logan said that for a moment he had a vision of the burning sidewalk not going out and the fire racing up the street like a bandit with a bag full of gold.

"I've seen fires in our city before." Logan laughed nervously. "But only in the instant when my own home was ablaze and the walk in front of my yard was alight did I truly realize how much wood there is in the city. Why, we are just a forest of dead trees, stacked up and nailed down and piled high."

Captain Logan spoke correctly that Chicago is

a city made of wood. At this date, the council reports that we have over 55 miles of pine block streets and 600 miles of wooden sidewalks, not to mention the majority of the buildings are constructed of wood, also. But the citizens of Chicago can rest easy, knowing that in spite of inevitable fires now and then, our water system, our fire alarms, and our brave firemen with their hoses and wagons can be trusted to keep even the worst blazes at bay.

George Rainey, *Chicago Tribune*
June 6, 1871

Madame Jocelyn was not as old as Methuselah, but she seemed to come close. She had thin white hair, which she covered with a bright orange hat held in place by a jeweled stickpin. Her wrinkled mouth and cheeks were boldly red, and she wore a corset so tight that Russell was amazed she could draw a breath.

He sat across the table from her in the Stick Saloon, sipping a cup of hot tea. Regular customers sat at other tables and at the long wooden bar, trying to sing along to the jarringly brash tune a girl was banging out on the piano. Alice Montague and Becky Alaimo were serving drinks. Smoke from pipes clung to the sooty ceiling like thunderclouds.

"I don't understand what you're asking, Mr. Cosgrove," the woman said, pursing her red, prunish lips and glaring. "You say you want to do *what*?"

"Open a place to serve those who live here. It's a charitable gesture, and I thought you might be willing to make a donation since these people are your neighbors."

"Have other saloon owners been approached?"

"Yes."

"And?"

"They've offered nothing, but—"

"I thought not." She lifted her cup and took a gulp. Russell could tell her tea was laced with something much stronger.

"There will always be the poor, Mr. Cosgrove. There's nothing we can do about it."

"That's what Pastor Botkins says. But I don't believe it."

"Oh?" One black-lined brow went up. "You don't?" She drained the remainder of her drink, belched, and call, "Becky! More for me! Mr. Cosgrove, sure you wouldn't like a bit of whiskey?"

"No, thank you."

"You sure?"

"I'm sure."

Russell thought he should leave. He'd been here nearly a half hour and she was no more willing than the other saloon owners to share her wealth. She might not be throwing him out into the street or threatening to knife him, but she was toying with him and that was just as bad. *One last try and then I'll go.* "I believe I've found a building," he said. "But I need a big table or two, and some chairs."

"Indeed," Madame Jocelyn snorted. "You are too handsome a young man to be worried about anything but young ladies."

Russell ignored this. "I need a cookstove and pots and utensils. I also need books, paper, pens, ink, clothes—cast-off but in decent condition."

Madame Jocelyn linked her fingers behind her head. There was a hole in the dress beneath her arm. "You sound like a missionary on his way to save a savage country. Glory, hallelujah!"

"That's exactly what I'm trying to do. But the savage country is right outside your doors, not in some far away jungle or desert."

Madame Jocelyn gave Russell a conspiratorial look. "Will it get me into Heaven, helping you?"

"That's not something anyone can answer." *This was a waste of my time and hers,* Russell thought. He stood up and bowed slightly. "Thank you for your time, ma'am. I'll be going now."

Alice Montague, dressed in a bright green dress and lopsided lace cap, came to the table with a decanter and poured Madame Jocelyn a nearly full cup. She waited until the old woman said, "And just what do you want?"

"I wondered if you'd heard about the dead woman," Alice said, glancing at Russell.

"What dead woman?" asked Madame Jocylen.

"Mrs. Brandermill. Beaten to death yesterday by her husband. Don't you know her husband, ma'am? I've heard you talk about him."

"Brandermill? John Brandermill!" said Madame Jocelyn. "In a world of lyin', cheatin' men, he's one of the worst. He'd kill his grandmother for a chew of tobacco!"

"I thought you should know that Mr. Cosgrove here tried to save the man's poor wife," said Alice. "Took her to St. Andrew's as she was dyin', to find help for her. Yelled at the reverend when the pastor wouldn't do anything to help. John Brandermill had beat her something awful."

"You tried to save John Brandermill's wife?" asked Madame Jocelyn, looking at Russell with one penciled-in eyebrow raised.

"Well, yes," said Russell.

"John Brandermill beat his wife and you tried to help her, out in front of God and everybody?"

"Oh, yes, indeed," said Alice.

"Most folks would have let her alone, knowing it was John Brandermill's wife, his handiwork. Good for you."

"Thank you."

Madame Jocelyn tapped her teeth, thought a moment, and then waved her hand. "Write out what you need. Any enemy of John Brandermill's a friend of mine."

Alice grinned broadly. Russell mouthed, "Thank you!"

Outside in the fresh air, Russell shook his head and smiled. "I'm going to get the supplies," he said in wonder. He looked back at the Stick Saloon and saw Alice peeking out of an upstairs window. She waved. He waved back. Then he set off down the street toward his apartment. *The next thing is to secure a place.* It wouldn't do to have a wagon dump chairs and pans in the road because he wasn't ready.

The air had grown humid with the onset of evening. It smelled like rain again. From open windows and sagging doorways, mothers called for children to come in for dinner. Men lit cigars on the side of the street while others retreated to the bright allure of the dance halls and gambling houses. Russell pulled his hands up into his sleeves as he rushed home to tell William the news. During the past weeks, this kind of weather had beaten him down. He had even begun to feel less than certain about his reasons for coming to this slum.

But tonight was different. Tonight, there was a friend waiting at home. For the first time in a month he didn't feel lonely. He felt, at that moment, that he could accomplish anything.

Russell went into the Sallee's shop before going upstairs. Lieutenant Sallee was behind the counter wiping his face on his bloody apron. The place was a mixture of sights and sounds. Sausages, bacon, and smoked fish were strung from the ceiling. In the shelves beneath the counter were chickens, unrecognizable chunks of meats, and tripe. Some was fresh and some spoiled; the combination gave off a salty smell that swam in Russell's head.

"Hello," said Russell. Lieutenant dropped the edge of the apron and looked up as if he knew something was wrong.

"Is there something the matter with the apartment?" he asked.

"No, not at all. I want to buy some meat," said Russell. "That chicken there. I'm celebrating tonight."

"Celebrating? You can't celebrate in my building!"

Russell laughed. "How much for the chicken, Mr. Sallee?"

The man snorted like a bull, and then pulled out the tray on which several plucked chickens lay. "Which one?"

Russell pointed. The butcher took out the meat and put it on the scale, saying, "You pay by weight, you know."

"I know."

"That's a four-pound chicken."

"Would you weight it again, sir," said Russell as pleasantly as he could. "Without pushing down with your thumb?"

Lieutenant snarled, moved his hand away from the top of the chicken and read the scale again. "Three pounds," he said. "And that was an accident, my thumb being there."

Russell paid for the chicken, went outside, and carried it upstairs. The lantern was not lit; the apartment was pitch-black. He put the bird on the table and glanced around, squinting. "William?"

There was a faint answer from the back room. "Here."

"What are you doing in the dark?"

"What do you think? I'm hiding. I heard someone on the steps and wasn't sure it was you."

Russell struck a match from the shelf over the stove, sending a brief whiff of phosphorus, then a glow. He touched the flame to the wick in the lantern.

There was a shuffling sound, and William appeared in the bedroom doorway. He still wore his coat and hat.

"You've been there all afternoon?"

"Only since it got dark."

Russell pointed to the bird on the table. "I bought a chicken to celebrate the successful day. Madame Jocelyn has offered to donate items for the safe haven. So, I thought, instead of my usual fare of bread and soup, we should have a feast tonight."

"Celebrate?" said William without smiling. "Why not? I'm stuck here, unable to go outside for a breath of fresh air until John Brandermill has forgotten me. Dandy!"

Russell felt a bit of a sting, and he sighed as he took off his coat. "What else can we do? If you can think of something, please tell me and I'll be glad to assist. Or leave, if that would make you happy. I don't want you beaten up or killed, but I'm not your jailer."

William looked at the floor. He seemed so vulnerable, with his hands crammed into the pockets of his trousers. Russell had the urge to go comfort the boy but didn't think such a gesture would be welcome.

"Would you help me cook, at least?" Russell asked finally.

"I better," said William. He looked up at last and tried to smile. "You nearly made me sick with that dreadful soup of yours. Who knows how much damage you could do to a whole chicken?"

9

Adam MacPherson stopped by at eight o'clock, ate a piece of the boiled chicken, and then agreed that, for two dollars and a free boot polish a week, Russell could use the theater. He made Russell promise to limit the number of people he would allow inside at once, however, fearing mobs might spilt the place down the sides.

"I'll be checking on you, to make sure all is well," Adam said. "You offer free food and there is going to be mayhem."

"I'll be sure the place is cared for," said Russell. "It will be hard, but I have to start somewhere."

Adam gave Russell an extra key to the theater, bid Russell and Katina a good evening, and left.

Russell waved his fork at the ceiling and cheered, "The plan is succeeding! I knew it would. I believe some things are mean to be and this is one of them. Your friend Adam is a fine fellow. I won't take his trust lightly."

"I hope it works out for you," said Katina. It was hard to listen to Russell's plans. Her thoughts raced back and forth like a dog in a cage, going over and over the same ground. *I've lost my job at Anderson's. I have no home to call my own. John Brandermill is looking for me in order to hurt me, maybe kill me!*

"To us," said Russell, raising his cup. Then he paused and gave Katina a long look. "I hope it is for us, not just me. You're trapped her for a while, true. And I know you've agreed to help me by writing only out of necessity. But I hope it becomes meaningful to you, too. When you see the faces of the old people, the children, William—"

"Don't call me that."

"Don't call you what?"

I'm Katina! "Nothing, I don't know. I'm so tired," she

answered. *Nobody knows the true me! The Monroe family on Michigan Avenue think I'm an insane woman with designs on their family fortune. Everybody thinks I'm a boy. What kind of life is this for me?*

"We're both tired. It's time for bed," said Russell.

Katina got up from the table, washed the dishes in a pan of warm water, used the brittle straw broom to sweep the floor, and then found a rag and began to wipe the table.

"Are you expecting President Grant?" asked Russell from the bedroom.

"No," said Katina.

"Enough, then. I can't bear all this cleanliness."

Katina put the rag on a shelf. Clearly it was time to sleep. *How am I going to manage that?*

Russell opened the bedroom window a crack. A cool breeze poured through and into the front room, countering the steamy air in the apartment. He called, "I don't have a wardrobe for your clothes, but I've got a trunk. You can put your clothes in there."

"I don't have many clothes."

"Maybe not, but they won't do all rolled up in your satchel."

The satchel! Katina instantly realized what was going to happen. She ran to the bedroom door and saw Russell unbuckling the satchel on the bed. "I'll put your clothes in the trunk with mine. They won't grow sour in there, I promise."

"No!" Katina dashed to the bedside and grabbed the satchel. "I don't want my clothes in the trunk."

Russell's eyes widened. "There aren't any mice in there, I promise."

"I don't care. I—I'll keep my things in here if it's all the same to you."

Russell shrugged. "Fine with me. Although it makes little sense."

It makes a great deal of sense to me! My skirt is in there, and my blouse, and my writings!

Russell lit the bedroom lantern, sat down on the bed, and took off his shoes. Katina turned to look out the window.

She could see the tainted haze of light that settled over the city at night. Light from candles in tenement windows. Light from lanterns in passing wagons or in the hands of nighttime pedestrians. Light from bows of the ships that rode the river to the west and north. Light from the frequent fires that plagued the city, burning down a shack here, a warehouse there, before the fire engines could arrive to put them out. The combined light rose above the city buildings in a vague canopy, mingle with the mist from the lake and blurring the stars and moon.

God, she thought. *Help me know what to do. I need something good for once in my life. I'm tired of fears and worry.*

"Are you coming to bed?" asked Russell.

She turned around. Russell was still on the side of the bed, his chest bare and his shirt folded neatly beside him. He was leaning forward, his arms resting on his thighs, fingers linked. His body was beautiful in the lantern light, with lines of fine muscles just beneath the skin of his chest and abdomen. She drew in a sharp breath, hoping he could not see her surprise or the sudden longing that had caused her heart to pick up its beat. Then she saw that his right arm was bandaged and that blood had seeped through the cloth.

"What happened to your arm?" she asked.

"Just a scuffle over at Bunch's Bar."

"Does it hurt?"

He shrugged.

Katina walked to the bed. "May I see it, to make sure it's healing properly?"

"And how would you know that, Master Monroe?" Russell gave a dubious smile, a strand of his dark brown hair filling into his eyes. Katina wished she could say, *Because the girls at Willowbrook were taught how to care for injuries.* But she only said, "I don't know. Let me look."

Russell slowly unwrapped the bandage, barely hiding a grimace as he did so. Katina said, "It's full of pus. Have you changed the bandage since you wrapped it?"

"No."

"Let me try something." Katina went into the front room, got a clean rag, and dipped it into the water bucket. She came back to the bed and, with Russell watching, began to wipe out the wound.

"Miss Innis had an unusual idea about the care of wounds," said Katina, feeling the need to talk to keep her mind off what she was doing. "She believed it was better to air out a cut and wash it often. She believed evil spirits came into a cut if it wasn't kept clean. She was quite the character."

"Who is Miss Innis?"

Katina's hands froze over the wound. Was there anything she could say to this man that wouldn't give her away? "Oh, an old friend. From long ago."

"Interesting," said Russell. Katina looked up at him. His head was tilted to one side his gaze questioning. "And you, William, are an interesting person. There's something strange about you, but I can't determine what it is."

Katina went back to work. Her throat felt tight, and she knew her face was flushed. She was touching him, holding his strong arm with its warm skin and surprisingly soft hair. Russell held still, breathing through his teeth, even as she dug deep into the blood-red wound to clean it out. It took two strips of rag to bandage it back up when she had finished. She tied the ends securely but not too tightly. Then she took the dirty rag back to the front room and rinsed it in the bucket.

"I'll toss out the water in the morning," said Russell.

"All right." She turned the wick down in the front room lantern, extinguishing the light. In the darkness, her heartbeats were all the louder in her temples, and it was all she could do to keep her breathing in check. She wanted to go back in his room and touch him again. She wanted to hold that arm, to put her head on that bare shoulder and to feel his own arms draw around her.

"I've given you my pillow," came the voice from the darkness in the other room. "And the blanket is plenty large. I promise not to kick you."

Katina stood still beside the stove.

"William? Have you run off?"

"I'll sleep out here on the floor."

"You must be teasing."

"No, I'll be fine. I can use my coat as a blanket."

"Why?"

She didn't know what to say. She went to the corner, curled up on the bare wood floor, and tried to snuggle down into her jacket. She removed her hat and balled it up into a worthless pillow. He would never touch her as she imagined. She had to know that, to accept that. Tears sprang to her eyes and she brushed them away.

"Why, William?"

She didn't answer. It was best to let him think she'd already fallen asleep.

Minutes later, there were footsteps beside her, a hand touching the top of her head, and the scent of Russell's cheap soap. He whispered, "You are a funny fellow, William Monroe. I hope someday to know you better." And then a blanket was being draped over her, there was one last pat on her head, and he was gone.

She lay in the dark with his blanket, feeling the tingle from his touch long into the night.

10

"I've named him Stump," said Russell as he put the little black puppy down on the floor, and the puppy immediately licked Katina's hand and wagged its wrapped, nearly nonexistent tail. "I rescued him from two teenaged boys outside the theater. They'd cut off his tail. I know he'll fare better with us."

Katina picked up the dog and buried her face in his soft, warm fur. "How dreadful, poor animal!"

"He can be company for you in your captivity," said Russell. He sat on top of the table beside the journal papers Katina had been sorting through all morning. She had read them all, but had only come up with a title: "A Case for Charity in Chicago." She'd written several sentences but had scratched them all out.

"I wish you could see everything Madame Jocelyn has sent! As I was clearing out the brush at the side of the building, a grumpy old gentleman came up in a wagon full of goods and told me Madame Jocelyn said he had to drive these over or she'd never let him step foot inside the Stick again."

Russell hopped off the table and began pacing back and forth. "There's a large oval table, terribly marred but with legs sturdy enough to hold a bear. There's an iron stove, some cast-off clothes from her working girls. Frilly, lacy things with rips from stem to stern but I think if we could find a lady good with a needle, we could transform some of it into suitable dresses."

"I see," said Katina. The daylight and Russell's enthusiasm lifted her spirits a bit, and she told herself she should be content now, at this moment, to be safe and cared for. To think about anything more would just make her miserable.

"Several pairs of shoes, lantern oil, a frying pan, and several cooking pots. Five wool blankets with barely a hole. Other things I can't remember. Some utensils. I've decided to call the safe haven Homeplace. Does that sound welcoming?"

Katina nodded and put the wiggling Stump on the floor. The puppy went to the water bucket and began to drink. "What now?"

"I've locked the theater. The place won't be ready until we've decided our next step. I haven't gotten any food at all yet, so we can't serve meals. We don't have paper or pens or books yet, so we can't teach lessons."

He's still saying "we," thought Katina. She found herself smiling.

Russell stopped pacing at her smile and his matched hers. "This is going to work, don't you think?"

"It will. There are few people with your determination. You amaze me."

"I do?" He came over to stand beside her and looked at the papers she'd spread out on the table. His hair had been combed earlier, but the wind had tossed it, and a few strands hung over one brow, giving him a carefree appearance. His eyes sparkled with cheerful purpose. "How is the writing going?"

"Actually, it's not, not yet, anyway," said Katina. "I've told you I write plays. The audience for this is educated, academic. It will be a challenge, but I'll do my best."

Russell put his arm around her shoulder. "I do wish you could come down to Homeplace and see what's developing. I wish there was some way, a trick we could use, a disguise to get you outside safely."

"A disguise is just what I need." She nearly laughed with the irony, but bit her tongue.

"Well," Russell said, moving away and picking up his polish box from the floor by the door, "I have to get on." As he pulled the front door open, a strong wind rushed in and blew Katina's papers across the tabletop until she dove on them. "I have to canvass the area and determine who we should first invite to Homeplace, the most needy. I need to polish a few shoes to buy some dry goods. And I plan on going by your old tenement house to see if Mr. Brandermill is still a free man. I'll be back in time for dinner."

Katina watched the door close, looked at the scattered papers, and then looked into the bedroom. A disguise, he had said. How could someone already disguised disguise himself—herself—and not be recognized?

Her pulse picked up.

"No, I can't," she told the puppy, who had found a mouse under the stove and was digging for it. "If I do, I can never go back to being William again. But why would that be so terrible?"

You can't be sure of what will happen if you do. You are safe as a boy. You have friends.

"But I don't have myself."

Stump barked at the stove then gave up and curled up in the corner.

"I am Katina Monroe." It was frightening, saying that aloud. She got up and took a deep breath. She picked up her satchel, opened it, and took out the blouse and skirt. Slowly she stepped out of her trousers and shirt, and walked naked into the bedroom, where Russell had a small looking glass on his desk. She held it up and stared at herself for a long time. This was who she was, not William the boy but Katina the young woman. And she was surprised to see her mother's beautiful eyes gazing back at her.

"In taking on a new disguise," she said to the woman in the mirror, "I will lose my disguise."

The afternoon was excruciatingly long. Wearing her skirt, blouse, and scarf, she sat at the front room table and made herself concentrate on the article. *If only I could make this into a play, she thought, I could do this.* A play about a child in Conley's Patch and his dog, and the rich man who came to his aid and saved his life. She could write something like that.

The hot, late June afternoon grew cloudy and humid. She lit the lantern, determined to ignore the noises from the street below, and tried to write. Stump woke, chewed at the bandage on his tail, and then went back to sleep.

There were footsteps on the stairs.

Katina dropped the pen and ran into the bedroom. She stood behind the door, waiting, listening. Was it dinnertime? How long had she pondered over the essay? She held her breath.

What will he think? The door unlocked with a rattle and then swung open. Katina watched through the crack between the bedroom door and its frame, feeling suddenly afraid.

What if he is furious at my lie?

"William?" called Russell. "Hey, Stump, where's William?" Russell glanced around, taking off his coat and dropping it on a chair. "You must be here, the lantern's burning." He shook his head. "Playing a game of hiding from me, then? Ha. How much of a game when there are so few places to hide? Under the bed? Behind the door?"

Katina cleared her throat silently and stepped out into the doorway.

Russell, who had been holding the dog, put him down slowly. He stared at her, emotions flowing across his face like waves on the lake. He said, "William, what an amazing disguise. It's incredible, it's just—" He stopped and then took a step forward. Katina did the same. The skin on her arms danced in trepidation and hope.

"Russell," she said softly.

Russell tilted his head in wonder. "It *is* a disguise, isn't it?" he asked.

Slowly, Katina shook her head.

"You…you are William, are you not?"

"For a time, I was," said Katina. "For more than a year now, after I came here from Georgia. But I've been acting. I had to, for reasons of safety, and then privacy. But now I'm in need of a new disguise, which means I can be myself again."

"Who…who are you?"

"My name is Katina. Katina Monroe."

Russell spun around and stared at the front wall. Katina could see his shoulders moving up and down with his controlled breathing.

"Do you think I'm ugly?"

"I don't know what to think."

"This must be quite a shock." *Oh, God, don't let him hate me!* "I'm eighteen," she continued, her voice steadier than she could have hoped. "My father died in the war, my mother and sister were burned alive on our farm. I've lived half my life in a home for orphans and then came to Chicago when I found reason to believe I have relatives living here."

His back still turned, Russell said, "But why disguise yourself as a boy?"

"You seem to understand the lengths people must often go to in order to survive. I came to Chicago after my family was destroyed. Yet my relatives here would have nothing to do with me, declaring I was a lying opportunist although I still have hope to someday win them over. But I had to make a choice. Boys on their own fare better than girls. Would you have had me work like Alice or Becky, at a saloon, doing all those…things… they must do?"

Russell said nothing.

"And yet it doesn't matter if you approve or not. I did what I had to do." As she spoke the words, she could feel her heart twisting inside out. It shouldn't matter what he thought, but it did. It mattered very much.

"I see," said Russell.

"I suppose it's done, then." Katina came into the front room, took her satchel from the chair, scratched Stump's ear, and said, "I've got your essay begun, though barely. Use it if you'd like, or start it over again. I'll be safe now. John Brandermill isn't looking for a woman."

She was moving for the door when his hand grabbed her wrist. She toward him and she could see his face had softened, so much that she wondered if he might have tears in his eyes.

"Katina," he said

"What?"

"I believe many things happen for a reason. Destiny, good and bad things, coming together to move us in the right direction. You didn't come here by mistake."

"No?"

He shook his head. "And I'd still like you to help, if you are willing."

"I'm willing to try."

He let go of her wrist, took a long, deep breath, and then shook his head and smiled. "I always thought there was something different about you. I just didn't know what it was."

Then to Katina's surprise, he reached out and stroked her

face and touched a loose curl of hair that hung loose from the scarf, not as an adult would touch a child, but in a new way. A way that made her breath catch and the flesh of her body stand at attention, waiting, hopeful.

He moved his hands to her shoulders and his face softened. She thought, *He's going to kiss me?*

But then he stepped back as if coming out of a trance and said, "You realize you can't stay her now, that's for certain."

"No," said Katina. Her words were shaky. "But I'll find somewhere."

"I know a place that is noisy, but there are two young ladies there who I believe would give you a bed if we asked."

"The Stick Saloon?"

Russell nodded. "But we'll make it clear you are only looking for a place to sleep, not a job!"

Katina said, "Of course not." She knew he was right, although at the Stick she would no longer see him every day. *It's all right,* she told herself, *He knows the truth. And he doesn't hate me.*

"Madame Jocelyn is tough," Russell said. "If I ask her, I'm sure she'll keep you safe from rowdy patrons. Her customers are afraid of her and she likes me."

Katina chuckled. "I hope they aren't too shocked to see me."

"I do, too. And Katina?"

"Yes."

"You aren't ugly. Quite the contrary."

Outside, the evening air was heavy with summer mist. Rain was on its way again. As Russell locked the door behind them, Katina wrapped her arms around herself and felt the air tickling her ankles. *Ah, boys' clothes are so much more comfortable.*

And then an arm took hers, and the touch was tender and as warm as sunshine, and Katina thought, *This may work out for the best after all. Things will never be the same, but I don't feel as afraid as I thought I would. Perhaps this is destiny. God bless destiny.*

11

Late July had settled on Chicago with an intensity that dried up all traces of mud and good humor, sent shadows fleeing into corners, and sucked the energy from every living creature. Horses hung their heads as if only their harnesses kept them standing, pigeons hid under eaves, and on the streets of the business district ladies tried their best, in vain, not to perspire. Rain was nowhere to be found.

Katina sat at the large table inside the MacPherson Theater with Bruce Charles, a nine-year-old girl named Carolina, and a pair of soot-covered twelve-year-old twins, Gregory and Gerrard Cruikshank. All the small windows were propped open to let in whatever tiny breeze might happen along, but the children were fidgety in the heat, and Katina had to struggle to keep her attention focused as well as theirs.

I'm not a teacher, she thought. *I'm no good at this.*

"Try again, Bruce," she said, pointing to a word in a book of poetry. "You know this."

Bruce shrugged. "Why do I want to read poetry? What good will it do me?"

"It doesn't matter what we read for practice," said Katina. "The point is to learn to read, whether a history book or a bill of sale. That way you won't be taken advantage of and you will earn respect. Try again."

Bruce rolled his eyes, making the other children giggle, and then looked back at the book. "Roses," he read in a halting voice.

"Roses grow upon the wall,
Borne on stems both green and tall,
Their blooms are lovely, red and sweet,
Yet their thorns a bane to meet."

"Fine," said Katina.

"We've read and done numbers for hours and hours today," said Gregory. It's too hot. Can't we stop?"

Katina shut the book, wiped her hand across her sweaty forehead, and said, "All right. I'll see you tomorrow. And no pocket-picking!"

The four children skittered out of the theater to the dusty street.

"You're good with them kids," said Becky Alaimo. She was sitting on one of the benches, snapping beans for the midday meal and dropping them into a bowl at her feet. Alice was next to her, shelling peas. Stump sat by the bowl, watching the peas fall in.

Katina pushed her sleeves up to her elbows, trying to cool off. She wore a dress that Alice had given her, one she'd had to modify so it was not quite so daring. She continued to wear a scarf around her hair, with had grown out an inch and was now puffy and hard to manage. "But I'm not, really," she said. "The safe haven has been open since the end of June. And it's nearly August. We serve a meal to thirty people a day, but turn twice as many away. We want to teach children, but I'm the only teacher and I'm not good at it. I thought we'd have a real teacher by now."

She went to the front door and stood holding the jamb and looking out through the dust. She remembered wanting to see no more rain. *What a stupid wish that was!*

"Where's Mr. Cosgrove?" asked Alice.

"He's taken the latest of my essays to the *Tribune*. This is my third try to get an article accepted, but I doubt we'll fare any better than the last two attempts. I just haven't the talent for essays."

"You sound bothered."

"I know I shouldn't complain," said Katina. "I've a place to sleep, thanks to Madame Jocelyn. I've work mending dresses for her, so there's a bit of money coming in. We have this theater for Homeplace, and only twice has someone tried to break in, and the only damage done was a couple splintered shutters. Children who have never set foot in a schoolhouse are learning a little, in spite of me. There are fewer people going to bed hungry at night."

"And," added Becky, "John Brandermill has at last been arrested for the murder of his wife, and he sits in the jail at the courthouse as we speak."

"Yes," said Katina. "But still—" She stopped.

But still, she thought. In spite of the growing conviction she felt for this place and the growing trust she was gaining in other people, she felt as if something were missing.

"It's Mr. Cosgrove, ain't it?" asked Alice.

Katina turned around. "Hmmm?"

"You're glum because Mr. Cosgrove won't pay you no mind, not like a man to a woman, that is. I can tell you fancy him. And I think he fancies you, too. But he ain't gonna say nothing."

"I—" began Katina. Alice was right. Ever since that night last month when Katina had revealed herself as a woman, Russell had continued to be friendly, but he had also begun to keep his distance. They had worked side by side for weeks, laughing and fuming over the creation of Homeplace, eating meals and working on the essays. At times they had shared a smile that seemed a little sweeter than usual, or they had brushed hands while moving furniture inside the theater, and she had felt a shiver of expectation and thought he had, too. But for some reason, he never let on.

"Tell me," said Katina, sitting down beside Becky and picking up a handful of peas to shell. "Why won't he say anything? He isn't shy by any means."

"Shy ain't the problem," said Becky, "It's something else. It's—" And then she stopped, nodded at the door, and whispered, "It's him."

Adam MacPherson stood in the doorway, grinning broadly and holding a battered book in his hands. "Hello, ladies! Simple Parker's wife gave me a geology book her son used to study, and I thought you could use it for the school." He came in and sat down at the table. He had obviously brushed his hair and tried to scrub the dust from his face.

"Hello, Adam," said Alice and Becky in unison.

"Hello," said Katina. She wasn't sure what she thought of Adam anymore. When he'd found out she was a girl, he had immediately banned her from performing with the theater troupe. No women, he'd always said, and he hadn't changed his mind. Katina was furious at first, but her anger had cooled somewhat because her attention was on Homeplace and the essay. As time went on, Adam had begun to come around several times a day. Katina sensed he had taken a fancy to her, in spite of the fact that she never did anything to encourage him. She found his attention bothersome.

"Where is everybody?" asked Adam.

"Are you looking for someone?" asked Alice. "Mr. Cosgrove ain't here."

"Good, I mean, I wasn't looking for anyone," Adam said. "I just brought the book. And I want to remind you that Pip, Chadwick, and I are performing tonight. Make sure the place is cleaned and empty by six."

"We always do," said Alice.

Adam scratched at his eyebrow. "Could I speak to you for a moment, Katina?"

"Now isn't convenient," she said. "The women's society will be here any minute."

"All well, then. Later, I hope," he said, standing. "You are taking good care of my theater, thank you. Good day." He tipped his well-worn hat and walked outside.

Katina let out a breath and shook her head slightly.

"That's why Mr. Cosgrove gives you a wide berth," said Becky. "He believes Adam is courting you."

"But he isn't! I don't want him to! What should I do?"

Alice just smiled.

The Homeplace Women's Society gathered twice a week at two o'clock—a handful of scarred, dirty, yet hopeful ladies of all ages who wanted very much to learn reading, arithmetic, and a bit of etiquette. Today, seven women and their ten babies came. As the women settled themselves on the benches and around the table, Alice made an announcement. "Miss Katina has helped us a lot, teachin' us things about books and manners. But today it's our time to help her."

The women nodded and Katina thought, *Oh, dear. What does Alice have in mind?*

The girls from the Stick Saloon called it a "gussying up party," and Becky whispered in Katina's ear that once Mr. Cosgrove saw how pretty she was, he would have to make a bid for her in spite of Adam. Katina protested, but Alice and Becky were determined. For the next hour, Alice combed Katina's chin-length hair into a semblance of curls, and as Becky presented Katina with a bright blue bonnet with a daisy pinned to the side, the women took turns offering advice about men.

"Don't laugh too loud," said one woman.

"Don't tell them what to do," said another.

"Smile a lot."

"Don't nag."

"Sit up straight. A man isn't looking for a woman with a bad back."

Katina didn't care for most of the advice; it seemed to turn women into creatures less important than men. And yet, she saw each of their eyes light up as they thought they were giving Katina something of value in payment for the lessons and food over the past weeks. For this, she appreciated their sincerity.

Then Becky opened a little bag she had with her and began to apply rouge in spite of Katina's protests.

"Oh, give this a chance!" said Becky. "I know what I'm doing. I do this all the time!" And so, Katina sat still as Becky rubbed and painted her cheeks, lips, and around her eyes.

When she was done, there were "Ahhs" from some of the ladies and frowns from others.

"Who has a looking glass?" asked Katina.

No one did, but there was a barrel behind the theater, and all the ladies trooped out after Katina as she went to see her reflection in the water.

"You're going to love it!" said Alice.

Katina looked in the water. She recoiled.

Her cheeks were brilliant red, as were her lips. Her eyebrows had been blackened and her eyelids were smudged with a sickly shade of orange.

"You look like one of us girls at the Stick!" said Becky with a huge grin of approval. "Now Mr. Cosgrove will see how pretty you really are!"

I have to get out of this gracefully, thought Katina. *Becky meant well but I look terrible! I can't bear to imagine what anyone seeing me on the street would think, much less what Russell would think!*

"I…I appreciate your trouble," said Katina as she and the women went back inside. "But it itches so. Let me wipe some off. Perhaps my skin would need to get used to any kind of beauty treatment before I could wear all this."

"All right," said Becky reluctantly. She handed Katina a handkerchief, and as the women collected their children and bid each other good-bye, Katina went back out to the water barrel and scrubbed her face vigorously. I didn't take long to remove most of the color, but a touch of it remained on her cheeks. Katina found the small amount surprisingly pleasing. It gave her the bit of color she didn't have due to spending so much time indoors. With the new bonnet and curls, she wondered if Russell might truly notice her and forget anything he suspected of Adam MacPherson.

"I'm running to Mrs. Savini's house," Katina told Alice, who had come outside to draw water for the upcoming meal. "She said she had a pig's head for us. I won't be long. I know you have to be back at the Stick shortly."

Mrs. Savini was an elderly widow who lived in a shack a block away. Her tiny house was falling down around her ears, she could never keep her pigs in their pens, and four times she'd been knocked on the head by men who'd broken into her home looking for something of value and finding nothing. Yet when she heard of Homeplace, she had made a point of finding ways to help.

Katina walked briskly along the bright, dusty street, heading for Mrs. Savini's home, wondering if she really looked better, wondering how many people would show up for the meal today and how many would be turned away, wondering if she should make one last visit to the Monroes and let them know she would visit them no longer, wondering so many things that she didn't realize someone was following her until she heard her name.

"Katina?"

She looked back. It was Adam, holding his hat, a few yards behind.

"Adam. What do you want?"

He smiled. "You look different. You look pretty."

"So," she quipped. "I don't usually look pretty?"

Adam came closer, his fingers fumbling with the hat. "I'm sorry. That's not what I mean. I like your bonnet and the daisy. Are you trying to impress someone?"

"I don't care about impressing others. Alice and the other ladies were just having a bit of fun with me, that's all."

Adam's face became serious. "I never went back to the work site after bringing the geology book today. I waited beside Skinner's Pawn Shop, hoping to catch you alone, to talk to you."

"Simple Parker is going to be furious."

"I'm not going to work for him anymore. I've tried out for a position with Steward Grand Theatre. I've got a good chance there, small roles at first but it's what I've wanted. Fame, remember? And soon, fortune!"

"I though you wanted to own your own theater."

"I have to be realistic. The MacPherson Theater is a dream that hasn't come true. I'll be accepted among great actors at Steward. Performing for the well-to-do! Katina, you're an excellent actor—actress—whatever. You don't need to be teaching ruffians, sewing for saloon girls. I could get you an audition, for the Stewart does accept respectable women on stage. Maybe they would look at your plays. We could have a wonderful time, out of this slum."

"I don't understand, Adam."

"Yes, you do. Don't play coy." Adam took Katina's arm. "I've become fond of you. I think you feel the same. Look how you've fancied yourself up for me." And he suddenly kissed her, a kiss that was passionate and insistent. A kiss that made her gasp and jerk away in anger.

And then she saw him standing behind Adam, holding her essay and staring aghast at the two of them through the bright sunlight that sparkled off the windows of roadside shops.

Russell.

12

"Let me go!" said Katina, pushing Adam away. "What do you think you're doing? You have no right!"

Adam looked stunned. "Katina," he mumbled. "I'm sorry. I...I thought there was no reason to hide my feelings now that I know you feel the same."

"But I don't!" she cried. "I don't care for you that way. And how dare you kiss me?"

"I didn't mean to offend you. Believe me, it's the last thing I meant to do, but I truly thought—"

Katina looked behind Adam again, but Russell was no longer there. *No, oh, no this didn't happen. He didn't see Adam kissing me!*

But clearly, he had. And he was gone.

"Just go away, Adam," Katina said. "Leave me alone. I'm sorry you felt misled, but I'm your friend, nothing more. Now, I need to fetch a pig's head!"

Adam gave her one last, confused look, and then stalked off down the street. Katina counted her breaths, trying to compose herself. *I can't let him think I'm in love with Adam,* she thought. *Forget the pig's head!*

With that, she gathered her skirts and raced back to the theater. Alice and Becky were standing at the stove, heating water for the vegetables and pig's head. On the table behind them lay Katina's essay.

"Where the head?" asked Alice.

"I don't have it!" said Katina. "Where's Russell?"

"He left, was only here a second," said Becky. "Said he had a boot-blacking job to do and didn't know when he'd be back. He requested you kindly handle today's meal on your own."

"Oh, God." Katina dropped to a bench. "I can't believe this."

"What's the matter?" asked Alice.

Katina shook her head. She didn't want to explain. It was too personal, and too embarrassing. It hurt her heart too much to speak of it. She didn't dare put the words on her lips.

"Do you want me to go get the pig's head?" asked Alice.

"If you don't mind," Katina managed. "I'm so shaky I don't think I can walk at the moment."

Alice left and Becky sat with her arm around Katina. "I don't know what's botherin' you," she said. "But I know that whatever it is, whatever ghost is chasin' you, it's always best to turn right around and chase it back. You never win, running away. It's like a dream, when a monster's comin'? You turn to him and yell and he disappears."

Katina nodded. She knew Becky was right. She felt a surprising surge of courage. "I should go right now. Can you stay a bit longer? No more than an hour, I promise. Get the meal going and I'll be back to finish. I won't let you be late for work at the Stick."

"If it's that important, then go."

"Thank you, Becky!" Katina ran for the door.

"It's about Mr. Cosgrove, ain't it?" Becky called after her. Katina said, "Yes!"

Where can he be? She wondered, holding her skirts and running down the middle of the gritty, potholed street. *What is he thinking? Where does he shine shoes? I know he works in the business district, but where exactly? There are so many streets!*

"Miss Monroe!" It was Bruce Charles, running behind her, waving his arms. "Where you off to? Is there a fire?"

"No," said Katina as the boy caught up to her. "Bruce, you shine shoes with Mr. Cosgrove on occasion. "Tell me, where does he set up? Where does he work?"

"All over," said Bruce, keeping pace with Katina. "Around State Street and Madison mostly, near the corner by a maple tree, not far from Archer's Millinery."

"Isn't there a main place?"

"Well, there is this maple tree—"

He told her the location of the tree and then asked if he could come along, too. But she said, "No, not this time. Listen to me, stay here. I mean it. Do you hear me?"

"That's not fair!" he whined.

"I'm sorry, Bruce, but you must do as I say." And without waiting for any more arguments, she ran off, hoping he wasn't following. He wasn't.

State Street was clogged with traffic, both on the street and the sidewalks. There were many trees along the street, as well, but Katina pushed her way through the crowds, seeking the one near Mrs. Archer's Millinery. Her bonnet strings had come loose and her hat slid back off her head. It bounced at her neck. She yanked it free and gripped it in her fist.

Please be there, Russell! If I don't find you soon I may lose my nerve!

She saw the millinery up ahead, with three prim ladies standing outside the door. She worked her way past with quick apologies and then spied the maple tree. The leaves were heavy and browning in the heat. And under the tree was a tall man with dark hair, wearing a white shirt.

Thank you, God!

She grabbed the man by the elbow. "Russell!" The man glanced over his shoulder. He had a thick mustache, sideburns, and red pimples on his forehead. He gave Katina a look of disapproval from behind his spectacles.

"Watch whom you touch, young woman!" he said.

"I'm sorry, sir! I was looking for the bootblack who often works beneath this tree."

"I've seen no bootblack. Now, go on about your business!"

Katina looked back and forth frantically. *What if he didn't go to shine shoes after all? What if he's decided to go away for a while? Would he do that to the people who needed him? Would he do that to me? Or does he even care that Adam kissed me? I don't know what to think!*

"I don't know!" she said aloud, and a lady nearby, stepping into a horsecar with her small daughter, glanced at her as if she were touched in the head.

And then she saw a man polishing the boots of another man across the street in front of a lawyer's office. The bootblack was kneeling down, rubbing the leather with a brush, as the man stood over him, looking at his pocket watch. Katina crossed the road, darting out of the way of carriages and jumping the horsecar tracks. The bootblack gave a final buff with the brush, stood, and took the coins handed to him. He stuck the coins into his pocket and began to pack the wooden box as the gentleman left.

Katina said, "Sir, you do a fine polish."

Russell turned around and looked at her. She couldn't read his face. It was sweaty and red from the heat, but his eyes were steady. "Hello, Katina," he said. "Is there something wrong at Homeplace that would bring you out here?"

"No," Katina said, realizing how out of breath she was, and how it hurt to breathe.

"Did someone send you to get me?"

"No."

"Then what have you run all the way here for? Did you want to know about your newest essay, the one I took to the *Tribune*?"

"Well, yes, I do, but—"

"They rejected it."

"As I suspected," she said. "But that doesn't matter right now."

"No?"

"Russell," she began. How to say this? She felt her head spinning, but her feet were secure on the e ground. "What you saw earlier, I wanted to explain."

"Earlier?"

"With Adam."

"Oh, that," he said. The corners of his eyes looked pinched with hurt, though he kept it from his voice. "Why should you explain? It's none of my business. I must offer you congratulations, however. I didn't realize how much your feelings for each other had grown."

"Russell, don't say another word. Not one! And listen to me." She slowly unpinned the daisy from her bonnet and pressed it into his hand. He looked at the flower but didn't pull away. "I do not care for Adam. He's a friend, but I've misread his actions these many weeks. It took Becky and Alice to point out to me that he saw me as a potential sweetheart."

Russell said, "I've thought that, too."

"I've been so busy becoming myself again that I was unaware of his behavior. I've loved writing the essay, even if each new version fails. I've loved working at Homeplace, even though I'm not a very good teacher. I'm learning to trust, Russell. That's quite a change for me. If only you knew—" She stopped. *If only you knew the truth, Russell. But how can I say it when I don't know how you'll react?*

Russell's fingers squeezed hers around the flower, ever so slightly. "Knew what?" he asked.

"That...that it is you I love," she whispered.

Russell's fingers tightened more firmly. "Katina, what did you say?"

She looked him full in the face. "That it's you I love, Russell Cosgrove, and no other."

Russell's face lit up and he dropped his polish box to the ground. He took Katina's other hand and said, "Katina, how I've wanted to say that to you. I've longed to tell you how wonderful you are, and yet there was Adam. Always Adam, everywhere. And now you tell me it isn't him that you love?"

She shook her head. There were tears in her eyes and this time she didn't wipe them away.

"You tell me it's true."

"Yes."

"And I love you, too," he said. "How much I love you!"

"But my essay is rejected again."

"I love you and your essay is rejected again!"

Katina laughed. Russell swept her into his arms and spun her around on the edge of State Street, while passing lawyers and financiers and shipping magnates and ladies looked on disapprovingly, but it didn't matter, none of that mattered, because she loved him and he loved her and the world was bright and warm and so very new.

13

Another Week With No Rain, Frolic Planned

The City Council has announced "Frolic by the Lake" for September 22, an event planned to take the minds of the citizens of Chicago off the dread, dry water that has plagued us since July. Bands are scheduled to play, and there will be games of badminton and croquet.

Only four brief showers have rained on our city in the past month and a half, causing late summer crops to fail, rain barrels to go empty, and tempers to sour. Streets are dust bins, and the elderly have experienced a high rate of lung diseases due to the dryness. There have been more fires in our city than in the last year, with a report of 613 at this date. With Heaven's help, there will come rain in the not-too-distant future. It would benefit us all.

George Rainey, *Chicago Tribune*
September 19, 1871

Adam MacPherson sold his theater at the end of September and told Russell and Katina that everything belonging to Homeplace had to be out by Monday, October ninth, when the new owner, a whiskey dealer, would move in. Russell suspected that the sale of the building had to do with Katina's rejection of Adam, and she agreed. Adam was hurt and he'd gotten a job at the Grand Theatre, so was washing his hands of his old home and old friends. He'd even found room and board with another actor who lived on the North Side.

The last meal for the poor was served on Saturday afternoon. Becky wasn't there to help because she was at the Stick, in bed with a fever. But Alice had come early to help prepare for the crowd; she looked as pretty as she could in a green dress, as if the last dinner should be a celebration. Russell and Katina decided that Alice was right; the meal should be joyous. They sent Bruce off in search of flowers, instructing him to ask for flowers from the street vendor on Griswold, not to steal them, while Russell went to Sallee's Butcher Shop to get some decent meat and Katina asked the pawn shop owner, Rolf Goltman, if he would play his fiddle.

Forty-three people were fed that afternoon, the largest number for any one day, and there were jars of purple larkspur to brighten up the room, German songs fiddled by Mr. Goltman, and an incredible meal of bacon, bread, cabbage, and apple pie. Men, women, and children sat at the large table, on the benches, on the floor, and outside by the dusty street. They gobbled up the food, shared scraps with Stump, and tapped their feet to the music.

Side by side at the stove, Russell and Katina stood with their arms around each other. Russell struggled with mixed emotions. Homeplace, which had been open for only five months, was going to close down, with not a single acknowledgement by the *Chicago Tribune* or a bit of help from anyone with wealth. He wanted to continue the work, but he would have to start from scratch. And yet here beside him, with her arm at his waist, was a loving, intelligent, beautiful woman.

Katina put her head against his shoulder and said, "Don't worry. We may not have a building but we've got the furniture and other goods. Madame Jocelyn said we can store everything at the Stick until we find a new place."

Russell kissed the top of Katina's head. "We do what we can."

The celebration went on until nearly six in the evening, with Mr. Goltman getting wild on the fiddle and people dancing in the road. Although the autumn had been brutally dry and hot, energy rose from the crowd like butterflies to the sky. Russell and Katina danced, too, but Russell felt clumsy and whispered apologetically in her ear that gracefulness was not a family trait.

At long last, Russell told everyone that he had to lock the building. The music and dancing stopped, and the men, women, and children faded away into the shadows of early evening.

Katina, Russell, and Alice cleaned the stove, swept the floor, then went out and locked the door. With the struggling Stump under one arm, Russell tugged the lock to make sure it was secure. He turned to find the two women.

"Oh," he said, pulling them both to him in a hug. "Nobody's died. We've lost nothing but our location."

They stood together for a long moment.

And then another woman's voice said, "Why, this is as lovely a sight as I've seen in a long time!"

The three pulled away from each other, and Russell stared at the lady in the tea cart who had spoken. She was dressed in satin, with her golden hair pinned up beneath a velvet cap. Her eyes were still as green as Irish shamrocks. Both the driver and the pony stared ahead with proper disinterest.

"Ellen," Russell said.

"Yes!" said Ellen Malloy. She opened the door of the cart and stepped out, and then carefully picked her way across the road. She took Russell's hand in hers. "Russell, I was so very glad you wrote to me! The letter was incredibly sweet. You know how I've missed you, our talks, our merriment, our walks. But oh!" She glanced about, wrinkling her nose. "I did fear for my life coming here. Men shouting from doorways, making lewd comments! And look at you, so much worse for the wear. But don't worry, we're together again."

Russell glanced at Katina. She was staring at the rich young woman with obvious apprehension. He knew how this looked, how bad it sounded. He prayed Katina would understand once he had the chance to explain.

Clearing his throat, Russell introduced Katina and Alice then handed Stump to Katina and said he needed a moment alone with Ellen. Alice said she had to go to work, and Katina shrugged and said simply, "Whatever you need to do." Then she leaned against the theater door with the dog in her arms and her jaw set.

Russell and Ellen walked to the corner of the street. Then Russell said as calmly as possible, "Why did you come here?"

Ellen dabbed her nose with her handkerchief, clearly uncomfortable with her surroundings. "You wrote me. You said you needed financial help to run this…this whatever you call it for the poor. You said you had tried to place articles about your work in the *Tribune* and were facing a long winter with little reserve. You hoped I would consider a donation in spite of our less-than-pleasant parting. Yet you expected me to send money to your parents' house without seeing you?"

Russell took a deep breath. "I wrote you for help," he said. "But I didn't mean to rekindle our relationship."

Ellen touched his arm. "We can do both, Russell. I've graduated from Brickmeyer's. I've not started up my girls' school yet, but I could use your help. Here's my idea. I will help you with your poorhouse if you'll help me with my girls' school."

"I can't."

"Why can't you?" She touched his cheek, and for a moment he remembered their first kiss and how warm he'd felt. But he pulled her hand way and said, "If you won't help me without stipulations, I must apologize for taking your time. And I must ask you to please leave."

Ellen made a *tsking* sound then said, "I admire your determination, Russell, but this is a phase you're in. I knew you liked to talk about social conditions but I didn't think you really wanted to get this involved. No one wants to live in a place like this if they have a choice. I'm offering you a choice. You know where to find me." She waved for the driver who brought the cart up close, then climbed in and waved good-bye.

Russell walked back to Katina, who was watching him with a steady gaze. "She was an old friend," he said. "She only came to talk about supporting Homeplace."

"You wrote to her for help?"

"Well, yes, I wasn't going to but—"

"You shared walks, you shared merriment with her? You wrote her an incredibly sweet letter?"

"It was a long time ago. I thought she might be willing to help. We have so little money. You do understand?"

Katina put Stump down. "She's very beautiful."

"I suppose."

"Do you love her?"

Russell knew he couldn't lie "I did. Once."

"I see."

"Listen," Russell said, taking a breath. "It's a fine evening. Why don't we talk a walk, or even catch a ride on a horsecar? No one needs us tonight. Is there someplace that would make you feel better, to take our minds off things? Let's take a stroll and clear our heads."

"I suppose," said Katina. But her voice was cool. *Hopefully,* Russell thought, a nice walk will help us both forget about Ellen's visit. *I know her life has been hard. I know she's lost so much and has had a hard time learning to trust.* He held out his arm for her, but she walked with her hands at her sides.

After depositing Stump in Russell's apartment, they meandered out of the slum through the business district. They said little to each other but Russell knew that at times silence could be healing. He knew he sometimes talked too much, rambling on when quiet was needed. When she was ready to talk, he would talk.

By the time they found themselves on Michigan Avenue by the lake, the sky was dark and filled with stars. A warm southwestern breeze tugged at their clothes. On the vast strethc of water, ship lights bobbed like fireflies. Couples and families were out enjoying the evening, strolling along the lane beneath the dense leaves of the oak and elm trees.

Katina suddenly stopped and pointed at a stone mansion within a stone wall. "There is my family," she said, "though they deny it. I've come here every other Sunday with a letter, and every other Sunday have been turned away."

Russell nodded. Beside him, Katina began to tremble. He put his arm around her waist and she did not pull away.

"A year and a half of trying," she said, staring at the house. "It's pathetic. It's more than pathetic, don't you think? To keep on? It's like a crazy woman, like a lunatic in an asylum, beating her head on the wall over and over again."

"It's not crazy to want something out of reach. How else would we ever gain something if we didn't try?"

She turned abruptly and walked across the wide street to where a short, wooden pier extended into the lake between the fenced yards of two stately mansions. A rowboat was tethered to the pier, and it rolled with the waves. Katina climbed onto the pier and strolled to the end, her skirt blowing in the wind off the water, her hands outstretched as if trying to catch something she desperately needed and desperately wanted. She tilted her head back like a drowning woman trying to find her breath.

Russell followed her and when he reached her, he took her upturned chin in his hands and said, "They don't know you or want you. But I do."

Katina's trembling grew stronger. But her voice was clear. "I need to let the Monroes go. There must be freedom in letting go."

"I think there is," said Russell. "We must let go of many things to move on. We have to let go of the old Homeplace to be open to the possibility of a new, better safe haven."

Katina whispered, "It's difficult."

"It is." He brought his face to hers; he ran his cheek along the soft curve of her nose, her cheek, her forehead. He took in the wonderful smell of her hair and skin. She sighed, almost inaudibly.

Writing Ellen for money was grasping at straws, he told himself. *But after the* Tribune *rejected all of Katina's essays, I panicked. But no more. I will work, I will move forward, and I won't look back.*

"I won't look back," he said. His lips found Katina's and she responded urgently. His hands moved from her face to her neck, and he kissed the gentle spot of her throat. Katina's fingers found his hair and caressed it almost painfully, then she pushed his suspenders down from his shoulders. Her mouth sought his again and the warmth and passion drew a moan from his lips. She whispered, "There must be freedom in letting go."

He closed his eyes as she feathered her fingers along his arms, pausing at the scar left from the knifing. Every fiber in his body awakened, longing to be touched by her.

"Love me," she said.

"I do."

She touched his eyelids and he looked at her. "Love me," she repeated.

"I will," he answered. His hands slid to her shoulders and she leaned into him, pressing against him with the whole of her body, and he pressed into her. Her breathing was faster now. The pier beneath his feet seemed to sway. Katina knelt on the pier, bringing Russell down with her. She looked up at him and what he saw in the sparkling starlight was the most beautiful sight in his life. "Love me," she whispered.

And he did. For their very first time, he loved her in the most intimate of ways. And she loved him back, fiercely, their bodies saying everything their hearts longed to say.

Morning came with a first hint of blue at the horizon across the lake. Waterfowl hovered around fishing boats that had gone out early for Sunday's catch. Katina and Russell, who had fallen asleep together, unlocked from each other, bringing on a wash of cool air.

Katina rubbed her neck and said, "I have to admit, I slept better last night than I have in months in the attic at the Stick. There was no fighting from below, no breaking glass, no Madame Jocelyn in a tantrum." She looked over at Russell, feeling a rush of awkwardness, hoping to see in his eyes the same love she had seen in them the night before.

And the love was there. The blue eyes regarded her with awe, respect, and tenderness. Katina felt her heart swell with wonder and joy.

They walked down Michigan Avenue, and Russell bought the two of them breakfast in a small restaurant near the Government Pier. They savored the bacon, toast, and oatmeal with molasses, even as Katina protested mildly that he'd spent several days' worth of his earnings as a bootblack.

It was the talk on State Street on the way home that first caught their attention, and then the gritty gray cloud hanging in the air to the west. They caught bits of conversation from people on the sidewalk.

"Huge, did you see?"

"All night!"

"Such a shame!"

"Worst fire in the history of the city," one gentleman was saying to another on the steps of a church as they held onto their hats in the wind. "With our city's alarm system and water mains, I'm surprised it got as bad as it did. Bunch of slovenly firemen on that poor side of town. Immigrants, you know."

Russell stopped and said, "Excuse me, sirs. What fire are you talking about?"

The two well-dressed gentlemen gave Russell a disdainful perusal, and then one said, "Where have you been, New York? Last night there was a fire on the West Side, over where the lumberyards and paper factories are. Burned four blocks around Jackson Street. Nearly made it across the river, and it took the firefighters sixteen hours to put it out."

"Yes," said the other man as he put the tip of a match to his cigar. "Quite a spectator event. We rode over there last night, watched from the Madison Street Bridge." He laughed as if it were nothing more than a curiosity.

"Heard drunks over on a block of Fifth Avenue went crazy last night, too," said the first man. "Set a few of their own fires. Burned a shop, another place or two. Like animals, riled up by the excitement. But at least," he added with a wink to his partner, "the fire stayed where it belonged and didn't bother the finer neighborhoods."

"Pompous imbeciles," said Russell as he grabbed Katina's hand and they quickened their pace for home.

"Fires on Fifth Avenue," Katina said. "I wonder where exactly? I wonder what kind of damage?"

Russell didn't answer, but something in the painful beating of his heart told him they wouldn't like what they saw when they got there.

They could smell the heavy, acrid haze from three blocks away, and there were still citizens moving up Quincy Street to the river to have a look at the damage on the other side. But it was the damage on their own block that made Russell and Katina stare in disbelief. They stood at the corner, hands over their noses against the sharp bite of smoke, staring at the spot where the MacPherson Theater had been. The walls were blackened and caved inward, dumping the shingled roof inside. The left side of the pawn shop next door was also burned away, and Mr. Goltman was in the road, wringing his hands. Several children Russell didn't even know were digging through the smoldering ruins with sticks.

"Do you see this?" Mr. Goltman wailed. "The fire last night on the West Side was an accident. But this fire wasn't! It was intentional!"

Russell stared at the charred cavern that had been Homeplace. Inside were all the books and furniture and clothing they owned, everything they were going to store then use to start again. Gone.

"It wasn't an accident?" Katina managed.

Mr. Goltman shook his head.

"Someone set it?"

The man nodded. "Heard a man named Brandermill got of jail a couple days ago, found innocent of killing his wife. Went on a binge last night with his buddies and tried to discover who'd told on him. Word this morning is that he found the undertaker who buried the wife and the undertaker described a boy who nobody's seen in months along with a tall, young man. Brandermill asked around and got the idea that the young man was you, Mr. Cosgrove."

Russell could barely speak. "He came after me?"

"Yes. Thinks you did it, you told on him, but I don't want to know if that's the truth or not, so don't tell me! But the man burned the stable—the theater—and Mr. Sallee's butcher shop, hoping you were upstairs, sleeping. Fire engines came, kept the fire from destroying other buildings, but you can see that the damage is done."

The butcher shop? God, no! Russell pushed past the pawn shop dealer and raced to the far end of the block. Mr. and Mrs. Sallee were sitting on a pair of burned chairs in the middle of the road, surrounded by an odd assortment of items they'd been able to get outside before the entire shop collapsed in flames. Mrs. Sallee was crying and rocking back and forth. Mr. Sallee was staring at the remains with fury in his eyes, as if he could resurrect it all with sheer will. When he saw Russell and Katina, the butcher jumped to his feet and swung his fist. "It was you he was after, Mr. Cosgrove! He wanted you dead! Now, see? See what your being charitable has accomplished? Nothing but bad!"

"I did not have John Brandermill arrested!" Russell shouted, pushing the butcher back. "But I would have done it if someone else hadn't! My intentions are to do what's right!"

"The road to Hell is paved with good intentions!"

"I never believed that!" Then Russell turned and looked into the burned, stinking maw that had once been a shop and his home. "Is there nothing left?" he asked as Katina held his arm.

"I don't think so," whispered Katina. She was shaking and her hands were clenched. "And Stump was in there! Poor little Stump!"

Suddenly, Russell climbed into the black, twisted wreckage and began digging. Splinters bit his fingers. And even though the fireman had hosed everything down, there were still red-hot fragments of wood that stung his palms.

"What are you looking for?" asked Katina. "Russell, it's all gone!"

"No, I won't let it be gone! There's something I must find. It will be a miracle if I find it, but it must. Just one thing!" His heart thundered with rage, grief, and frustration; his hands clawed for a recognizable remnant. He dug through burned bits of meat, wet, ashy scraps of clothing and curtains, broken jars and pottery, an upturned cookstove, a smoldering shoe.

Katina watched silently from the road. Mrs. Sallee continued to cry and Mr. Sallee said he was off to have a drink at the Stick, there was nothing for him anymore.

Then, beneath an upturned slab of smoking wood that had been part of his desk, he found it.

"Yes," he whispered.

"What is it?"

He held the Bible, still intact, to his chest and climbed back out to the road. "I've found it," he said in wonder. "This precious book and all that is inside."

Katina took the book from him. "A sign of hope?" she said uncertainly. "A place to start."

And then her face went hard, and she stared at the road. Two small envelopes had fluttered from the pages. She stopped to pick one up. "Oh, Russell…" she began.

"No, Katina, let me explain," said Russell. *How could I have forgotten they were in there?*

Katina glanced up at him and the look was a lance to his soul. "These are two of her letters," she said slowly. "Ellen's letters, aren't they?"

"Yes, but—"

"You said, 'This precious book and all that is inside.' You hoped to find her letters unharmed. They mean that much to you."

"No, Katina."

"*She* meant that much to you." Katina's eyes were brimming but her words were controlled.

Russell reached for her, but she pulled away. "Let me explain. You must trust me!" He knew his words sounded harsh but he was so tired, so angry, so defeated. Couldn't she see what had happened? It was all gone, burned into nothing. "It wasn't her letters I hoped to find!" He took the Bible from her and quickly flipped through the pages. *It must still be in here. Where is it?*

He looked up to see Katina backing away, hold her hands out in resignation. "I did trust you. Completely."

"Katina, wait."

"I'm going," she said simply. "I don't want to talk now. I need to be alone. I don't understand what all this means, Russell, and it hurts too much to consider. But you agreed there is freedom in letting go. Perhaps there is freedom from heartache!"

"Wait. Katina, it's you I love. That's all there is to understand."

"Don't follow me!" she said, holding up her hand. She turned and walked off, her head defiantly high.

"I'm going to see my parents on De Koven, then!" he called after her. "In case you want to know!"

She turned the corner without looking back.

"In case you want to know," he repeated to the empty space she had filled a moment ago.

He sat down beside Mrs. Sallee and handed her the Bible. "You may want this more than I do," he said. "I pray you and your husband find peace. I cannot imagine at this moment that there is any for me."

She looked at the Bible in her lap, sniffed loudly, and opened the cover. "I can't read," she confessed.

Russell reached over and took out what had been stuck to the inside front cover, that which he hadn't seen when he'd flipped through the Bible. It was the pressed daisy Katina had given him on the first day she said she loved him. It was what he'd meant when he said there was something precious inside, not Ellen's rambling missives.

For a moment he thought of chasing after Katina, but he knew her temper. He also knew that he, too, was angry because she hadn't trusted him and had immediately thought the worst.

All was destroyed. His home. His dreams. His sweet little puppy. His true love. Her trust.

And so, he took the dried daisy, put it into his shirt pocket, rubbed the soot from his hands as best he could, and began the long walk to his parents' home on the West Side across the river.

14

It was always difficult to tell what time it was from the windowless attic bedroom in the Stick Saloon. Although most of the rowdy drinking and gambling was two floors down, it was constant and loud, as raucous in early morning as it was at 2 a.m., breaking only when Madame Jocelyn got in a snit and kicked everybody out.

Katina had fallen asleep not long after leaving Russell at the burned-down shop, climbing the narrow steps to the attic from the second floor and dropping to her cot in a fit of tears. *It cannot be worse than this,* she had thought. *Homeplace is destroyed. What I thought I had with Russell is destroyed. My family doesn't want me. Why must I always be betrayed? And now there is nothing left to lose.* She had cried, then cried again, until sleep pulled at her and took her into its soft, motherly arms.

But then Alice was at the door calling, "Katina! You have to get up and see it!"

Katina opened her eyes, blinking. It was pitch-dark, with a slice of light from Alice's lantern beneath the door. "What is it? I really want to be alone."

"It's started again," the girl said. "We're all going to the bridge to watch. Don't you want to come, too?"

"What's started?"

"Another fire. On the West Side. This one is even worse than the one yesterday!"

Alice didn't wait for Katina to get up. She opened the door, and the light startled Katina to full consciousness, causing her to blink madly.

"Are you sure it's not the smoldering from Saturday's fire that looks like a new fire?" Katina asked.

"Can't you hear the bells?"

And through the thin walls of the attic, Katina could indeed hear the clanging of the distant Courthouse bell, and the fainter, accompanying sound of church bells. This was a true alarm.

"There's always a fire somewhere, Alice. I have more things to worry about than someone's burning tool shed." She pulled her pillow over her face.

"This is much worse! I looked outside already!"

"What time is it?"

"Quarter after ten or so. Come on!"

Katina removed the pillow. "What about Becky?"

"She's still sick in bed. She'll be fine. We'll be back when the fire's out and she'll never know we're gone." Katina slipped out of her nightgown and into her dress and shoes.

Downstairs, the saloon was empty except for Madame Jocelyn, sitting at a table, smoking a cigar. "They've all run off and left me!" snarled the white-haired woman. "Think it's more of a lark to watch a fire than play cards with me? Fine, I'll shut the place down for a few hours, see how they like that!"

"We'll be right back," Alice offered tentatively then dragged Katina outside by the hand.

In the street, the wind had picked up, and the crowd was clutching skirt hems, jacket collars, and caps, pushing eastward toward the river, their chatter anxious and loud. The boarding houses and saloons lining the street had lanterns blazing in windows, making the road seem nearly as bright as day.

"I heard someone say it was nine blocks gone already!" shouted one woman to another as Katina and Alice stepped onto the rutted road. "Can you imagine? What do you think we've done for God to pass such judgment?"

"Ain't judgment," said the other woman. "It's this dry weather and this wind! All the water in the world can't put out a strong wind!"

"Nine blocks!" said Katina, grabbing Alice's elbow. *Russell is on the West Side with his family. He surely can't be in the path of the fire!* "Do you think that's true? I can't imagine such a blaze!"

"Me, either," said Alice. She and Katina picked up their pace. "Let's get to the Madison Street Bridge. We can best see from there."

A man bumped into Katina, and then another, giving no apologies but pushing around and ahead. The others in the crowd seemed oblivious to the shoving. There was entertainment ahead, regardless of how grim, and they wanted to get to the river faster than the others to find a good place from which to watch.

"Look at that sky!" said Alice.

Across the river and to the south, the sky was pulsing orange and red. Flames could be seen intermittently, leaping upward in tremendously tall red fingers somewhere beyond the still smoking remains of lumberyards and factories from Saturday's blaze.

It looks like war, Katina thought as she and Alice stumbled onto the end of the bridge and stopped, unable to go farther because of the crowd. *It looks like what the renegades did to my home in Georgia, magnified over and over!*

Madison Street Bridge was already crammed with people, pressed against each other, clutching the railings, shouting and pointing at the sight. Children shouted, laughed, and ran about as if they were at a party. Police officers had placed themselves in the midst of the commotion, some on foot and others on horseback, but they seemed as curious as the rest in what was happening over in the West Side, and did little to deter the crowd. Rooftops along the river's edge were also lined with others, who had climbed up to watch. The wind-churned water of the river reflected the terrible inferno to the southwest, its waves shimmering with red and gold. Barges and small steamboats moved as quickly as they could up the river, trying to escape what could be their doom if the fire wasn't halted. Although this bridge—like the others that spanned the river—was capable of being cranked and turned away from the banks until it was parallel with the river in order to let larger ships pass, it remained in place across the water as the curious crammed onto it. Sailboats and other taller vessels would have to wait until the bridge was turned to get out.

"Does anyone know where the fire started?" Katina shouted. No one answered. "Where did it start, please, I must know!" A woman turned and stared at her then passed the question up the line along the bridge. A minute later, an answer was passed back. "Someone says Clinton Street. Someone else said De Koven!"

Katina's knees buckled. It felt as though someone had punched her in the chest. Alice caught her. "Katina, don't you faint on me!"

"Russell's over there," Katina said. She drew in all her strength and pushed herself upward, locking her shaking legs beneath her. "Russell's visiting his family! They live on De Koven!"

"Sweet God, do you think he's dead?" Alice asked in a hushed, horrified whisper.

"Don't say that! Don't even think that!" She looked ahead at the thick crowd on the bridge. It would be hard to get through, but she had to do it. She had to find Russell. She had to make sure he was safe, that he was not in danger. And she had to tell him she was sorry, so very sorry! She knew the letters didn't mean anything to him, not really.

I've been distrustful for too long, she thought. *Yet he's been so caring, so patient. I have to tell him I was wrong not to hear him out today! I have to tell him that I do love him. I have to find him!*

"Alice," she said. "I've got to go find him."

But Alice gave her a sharp shake of the elbow. "No! It's too dangerous!"

"It doesn't matter!" Katina turned sideways, and tried to push her way through the gaping crowds, but angry people shoved her back and out of the way. *I love him,* she thought. *He said the letters meant nothing. I believe he was telling the truth. If I had not been so stiff-necked, he would still have been on Fifth Street, where it's safe. It is my fault he is in danger now!* She tried to push forward again and one fat, sweaty man lifted her and dumped her back. "I have to get through to the other side!" she cried, but no one seemed to care.

"Katina!" came a small voice. It was Bruce Charles, not far from Katina, clutching the side of the bridge. He was grinning broadly. "Ain't it exciting?"

"It's not exciting!" she shouted. "It's dreadful! All those poor people, and Russell in the middle of it!"

"Russell's over there?"

"Yes, and I have to find him!"

"I'll go, too!"

"No, Bruce!" said Katina, but of course, Bruce didn't listen. He let go of the railing and grabbed Katina's hand. "Give us room!" he said to those around him. "Lady with consumption here, let her through!"

The people nearby gave Katina a disgusted stare then stepped away far enough for the two of them to move forward. "Got consumption, get out of the way!" said Bruce. People cringed and moved against each other to let them pass. Katina added effect by coughing loudly.

We'll get over the bridge, Katina thought, *then stay to the riverbank as best we can, climbing grain elevator and factory fences when we have to! De Koven is south, I know that. We will find him! Oh, God, let us find him!*

"I think I see St. Paul's steeple," yelled one man on the bridge. "Yes, that's up, burning like a torch!"

"Incredible!" shouted another.

How could anyone think watching this is sport? thought Katina. *It's horrific!*

There was the clang of fire engines bells coming from the east, and the people on the bridge crushed themselves together to let them pass.

"It must be a dreadful fire, for sure," said Bruce. "Extra engines from our side goin' over to help!"

Three horse-drawn steam engines from South Side fire departments clambered onto the bridge, forcing their way through the spectators. Clouds of steam and cinders hissed from the engines' boiler huge stacks, and a fireman running alongside shouted at the people through his brass speaking trumpet. "Get off the bridge! We are needed, space is needed, let us through!"

Some of the crowded backed up, although many people just pressed themselves together more tightly, hell-bent on keeping their places. Katina could no longer move forward; the crowd was too tight.

Someone cried, "Oh! It's crossed over to South Side!"

And it had. The wind had blown ash and chunks of flaming buildings across the water. About a quarter mile down the river, flames could now be seen on both sides. The curious expressions of the spectators began to fade as they realized what was happening. If they wind kept up, their homes would be next. There was gasps now in the crowd, and some women screamed.

"Bruce!" Katina said. "I'm going across on the railing."

"You aren't!"

"Yes, I am!"

Slowly, she pulled herself up onto the wide, flat bridge railing and clung to it on hands and knees. All she had to do was crawl to the other side, about twenty yards away, and not look down. The water was thirty feet or more below, and she could not swim. *I'll make it,* she told herself, her heart pounding. *I've got good balance, I'm strong!*

If only I was still in the boy's clothing I used to wear!

Suddenly a fourth steam engine crossed the bridge, its horses snorting madly, and the crowd caused it to careen off path. The side of the engine struck the railing and dragged at it for a moment. Katina was face to face with a terrified fireman at the reins, who reached out for her at the last second, but it was too late.

The impact threw her knees out from under her, and she was falling over the side of the bridge, her arms flailing, her hands grasping nothing but air, until she struck the water with a force that knocked her breath from her body, and she was sucked down into the cold, and the wet, and the black.

15

Russell had gone for a walk Sunday evening in his old neighborhood, after having a meal with his parents in their cottage on De Koven and telling them about the destruction of Homeplace. However, he said nothing about the way he and Katina had parted. His mother had given him an extra serving of squash to make him feel better. His father had taken him out back to show him how the dry weather had killed his crop of pumpkins then had put his arm around his son's shoulder and said, "You come from strong stock. Our family has always survived whatever has been put in our way."

Russell had thanked his father for the encouragement, but had not felt encouraged. Not bothering with a lantern, he left his parents' house at nine o'clock in his canvas coat and strolled east along the dark, dusty street, past the ramshackle cottages with their unpainted fences and cluttered yards. It was obvious from the dark windows that most of the neighbors were in bed. The wind was steady from the west, blowing grit and dry leaf crumbs in Russell's face.

He sat down on the edge of the road outside the O'Leary family house, pushed up the sleeves of his coat and took the pressed daisy from his pocket. He looked at it and then at the hands that held it. Hands had a great deal of power, power to help, power to hurt. Leaving like he had this afternoon was wrong. Not going after Katina to show her the flower and to assure her of his love had been cruel. She'd been hurt so much in her life. He wanted to be part of her healing, not part of her pain. Although the night was warm, regret ran cold beneath his skin.

"Tomorrow morning," he said as he put the flower back into his pocket. "I'll return to The Stick. I'm going to tell her I'm sorry and ask her to marry me."

"What's that?" came a voice nearby. He looked down the road to see James Dalton, a neighbor, standing near the road in front of his house, smoking his pipe.

"Just woolgathering," said Russell.

"Mmm-hmmm," said James, and he went back to his pipe.

Russell looked up at the leaves flying over his head like silent ghosts. *Such a thought, marriage.* He would not have fathomed such a thing was possible six months ago. *But now it seems right. To have her and hold her.* He would have someone to rejoice with, someone to hold and cherish when the world turned harsh.

"If she will forgive me," he said quietly. "Dear God, please let her forgive me!"

He smelled it at the same moment he heard the shout behind him, "Fire, fire!" Russell jumped to his feet and turned to see tongues of flame licking out from the windows of the barn behind the O'Learys' house. And then Peg-Leg Sullivan, a neighbor with a wooden leg, was running across the O'Leary yard and pointing. "The barn! It's gone up! We have to wake everyone! I'll get the cows!"

As Peg-Leg hobbled behind the O'Leary house and yanked open the door to the burning barn, Russell took the O'Learys' front steps two at a time and pounded on the door. He knew from his mother that this section of the house was rented to Patrick McLaughlin, and Russell could hear the McLaughlin family inside, singing and talking. "Fire in the barn!" he yelled. "McLaughlin, there's fire out back! Get out!"

The singing stopped and Mr. McLaughlin called, "What?"

"Fire!" repeated Russell. Waiting no longer, he jumped from the porch and was joined by James Dalton. They then ran around to the side door, which was the entrance to the O'Learys' part of the house. "Fire in your barn, wake up!" shouted James through the shuttered window.

"Get out now!" cried Russell, banging on the door.

From the barn, Peg-Leg emerged, hopping without his wooden leg, clutching the neck of a wild-eyed calf. Smoke and flame billowed out behind him, and flames had broken through the roof. Thick showers of sparks rode the wind to the James Dalton's yard next door. "Horse and cows are burned up!"

Peg-Leg shouted to Russell as Russell helped the man away from the barn. "Lost my leg in a hole, couldn't stay to pull it out. This blaze's going to travel fast!"

Patrick O'Leary opened the door of his cottage and stared in horror at the burning barn. "Catherine!" he called into the house. "Get the children, there's fire!"

Neighbors had heard the shouting and were quick with buckets and pans of water from their wells and pumps. Women, children, men, and old people converged in yard, tossing the water onto the barn, which was clearly past saving. The O'Learys' roof was smoldering now, and the dry grass in Mr. Dalton's yard had ignited. Russell joined the brigade from the O'Learys' well to the blaze, hauling up buckets full of water and passing them down the line. Water was tossed up onto the O'Leary roof as well as the barn. But he knew the efforts were futile. There was no way citizens could stop this on their own. It was spreading too quickly. Embers had blown from the Dalton yard onto their roof and had caught the house on fire. They also landed on the shed roof and dry garden of the home next to that and took hold.

"I'll alert the fire department!" Russell called.

"The nearest alarm box is at Bruno Goll's drugstore on Canal!" called Patrick O'Leary as he tossed a bucket of water against the side of his house and it sizzled immediately into steam.

A block away from the drugstore Russell met Robert Lee, who was returning from Canal Street, panting and wheezing. "I've gone about the alarm, if that's where you're running to," he said. "Mr. Goll wouldn't give me the alarm box key. Said he would telegraph the alarm himself. The engines should be here soon, I pray God!"

"He refused to give you the key?" Russell asked. This was odd. Citizens had the right to get the alarm box key and send the message to the central dispatch office at the Courthouse themselves.

Robert nodded. "Mr. Goll seemed perturbed that I disturbed him. Woke him up, interrupted a game of cards, I don't know. But he promised to send the alarm."

"I hope you're right!" said Russell, turning back toward the O'Learys'.

Russell's mother and father joined the crowd on De Koven, stoically assisting with the dousing of the fire with buckets they'd brought from home. Every nearby well and rain barrel was put to use, but hauling the water and carrying it to the flame was slow and awkward. Much water was splashed and lost. Two men hoisted a full barrel onto their shoulders and dumped it on the porch of James Dalton's now-burning porch. Russell felt a surge of pride in these brave people. He passed yet another bucket of water to outstretched hands as the heat from the ever-growing fire made the skin on his face singe.

Neighbors for an entire block past the O'Leary house were out of their homes now, most dragging everything of value into the streets in fear their own homes were next. Tables, chairs, mattresses, cooking utensils, all piled in the middle of the road with children huddled among them. Some began to load wagons to escape if they had to, but Russell knew that because of the poverty of this area many people did not own wagons, or horses, and if they had to get away, it would be done on foot.

"Where are the blasted fire engines?" shouted Patrick O'Leary. His own children were in the street with neighbors' children. "It's been twenty minutes! They should be here!"

But they weren't. The fire, urged by the relentless wind, blew across the backyards to Taylor Street, setting several rooftops ablaze. Some De Koven residents followed with their water buckets.

Russell knew the only hope was the fire engines, which, incredibly, had still not appeared on the scene. He shouted to his parents, "I'm going for the engines again!" and ran the three blocks to the drugstore. He slammed through the front door and found Bruno Goll inside, calmly counting money behind the counter. Russell shouted, "There's a fire on De Koven! Have you sent an alarm?"

Mr. Goll sniffed. "What? Oh, yes, I did not long ago."

"You are certain you did?"

"You call me al liar?"

"Then give me the key," said Russell. "We need to send another alarm!"

"No, I've seen an engine pass. They're on their way."

"Then the engine driver must be confused, because the engine hasn't come to De Koven!" Russell felt anger in his chest as hot as a fire.

"The alarm's sent!" insisted Mr. Goll. "Now get out, I'm going to lock up to watch the fire myself!"

Russell wanted to grab the man and shake him for the key, but of course the man was telling the truth. He had no reason to lie. Shoving out through the door, he was met by a group of people heading toward De Koven to see the blaze. Russell hurried with them to the intersection of De Koven and Clinton Street, and drew up in shock.

The fire had spread drastically, with still no sign of the fire engines. The O'Learys were at the end of the block, staring back at the blaze that had consumed part of their house and most of the homes of their neighbors and was now burning the very ground on which the homes had stood as well as some of the furniture abandoned in the middle of the road. Robert Lee's family had found an empty lot on the south side of the street, and they stood in the dry grass, clinging to each other and to Patrick O'Leary's shivering calf.

"It happened so fast!" Robert called to Russell. He had his arm around his wife, and they were both crying. "If something isn't done soon it will be as bad the one Saturday night!"

"No," said Russell. "That couldn't happen!"

"It could, Russell!"

Spectators rimmed the sidewalks of Clinton, pointing and staring as shanties, sheds, and trees went up in a progressively rapid succession just a half-block away. Russell pressed through the thick of them, trying to get ahead of the blaze. "Won't someone come with me?" he shouted to the crowd. "Folks up ahead are going to need warnings and help!"

One blond young man answered, "We're into an adventure, we'll come, won't we, Paddy?"

Paddy, a short boy with bristly hair, said, "I'll be a hero, you just wait!" And the two ran after Russell, cheering and laughing with each other as if they were off to the cockfights. Russell didn't slow down; if they meant to help, they would keep up. The fire had set a dreadful pace, like a sprinter hell-bent on winning some sort of ghastly race, but he would give it a run for its money.

At last there was the sound of fire bells clanging and horse hooves clattering over the noise of the fire and wind and shouts. Two engines passed on the street, one a hose cart that could only throw water short distances, and the other one was an old, out-of-date steamer. They were headed for De Koven, but Russell knew they had a job ahead that would require five times as many engines.

Russell and the two young men crossed Taylor street, dodging panicked goats, pigs, and carts people in the middle of the intersection. Overhead, the wind carried blazing debris like kites on the air. Russell felt sparks land on his neck. He batted them away and pushed ahead.

Three blocks up the fire was still speculation, but most of citizens were already in the road with their furniture and clothes, some in wagons with harnessed mules and horses, ready to flee. They stared at the approaching smoke and flames, yelling to each other, "Fire engines are on their way. They'll get it before it reaches us, God willing!" Several little girls, clearly trusting in their parents' stoic manners, played hop-scotch in the road dust, giggling with each toss of the pebble.

One stooped, bearded man was in his yard behind his wobbly fence, clutching a yellow kitten. Russell called over the fence, "Sir, we're here to help you get out. There are only two fire engines fighting the blaze at the moment. We cannot take a chance! It is traveling much faster than you can imagine!"

The bearded man eyes turned in Russell's direction, but his head did not move. "It don't dare come bother me," he said. "Fire come last winter and burned my house down good and flat. Built it up again with help of my sons. It don't dare come after me again. I just won't let it, you hear me?"

"He's crazy!" one woman in the road shouted to Russell. "He won't listen to reason, never has!"

The blond man with Russell said to the old man, "I see

you've got a hand cart there in the side yard."

"We'll help you pack," offered Paddy.

"No," said the old man. "Fire don't dare bother me!"

"Sir," Russell tried again. "I hope you're right. But it does no harm to be ready."

"He's a lunatic," called the woman in the road.

From down the block, there was the sound of more fire engines coming to the scene. *Four more, maybe five,* Russell estimated. *That's still not enough!* A man ran from behind a house on the south side of the road, waving his hands wildly and crying, "Get out, get out! I seen it comin' and it's the devil's work! Fire engines are pumpin' all they can, but the water just boils away! Get out!"

As if to prove the man was right, there was suddenly a burning shirt in the air, flying over rooftops from the direction of the blaze, its arms outstretched and flapping. It landed on a dead shrub in the old man's yard, and the shrub went up with a whoosh.

"Sweet Jesus!" cried one woman, and the rest of the residents joined in her screaming heavenly appeals. There was a scramble into the wagons and a grabbing of reins and whips. Those without wagons hoisted their trunks onto shoulders and snatched up the bundles and boxes as best they could. As they rambled and pushed toward the end of the road, Russell heard, "Never thought it would come this far! God be with us!" "Hurry, Maybelle, and don't drop that doll for we shan't come back to get her!"

Russell, Paddy, and the young blond man stood in the road, staring at the old man with his kitten as his shrub burned like tinder in a fireplace and sparks fell to his grass and began to smolder.

"Come with us!" Russell called firmly. "We can't let you die here, sir."

"We'll drag you out if we have to. Sir," echoed Paddy. Russell could hear the uncertainty in Paddy's voice and could feel the uncertainty in his own gut.

The old man stroked the kitten's yellow fur, looking not at the three men in the road but at the golden night sky to the south. His long white beard blew around his face in the wind. "Been pushed around my whole life," he said. "Always been told what to do. My wife. Bosses down to the train yard. Last year, fire told me to get out of my house, it was gonna burn it down. But not anymore."

Russell knew the only thing to do would be take the man by force. "May I hold your kitten?" he asked slowly.

The old man continued to stare at the sky, but he began to move backward toward his house. More red embers began to drift down around them.

We have to hurry!

"Let us hold your cat, sir," said Paddy.

"Don't tell me what to do," growled the old man. An ember landed in his beard and began to smoke.

"Please!" said Russell, running over to the man and waving his arms. "Sir! We only want to help!"

The old man turned more quickly than Russell would have thought possible, ran inside, and slammed the door. Russell and the two men raced through the gate and beat on the door. It was locked tightly.

"Curses!" said Paddy. "What do we do now?"

A larger piece of flying, burning debris landed at their feet. The air was stiflingly, suffocatingly hot. "I know what I'm doing," said the blond man. "Enough of this lark, I'm no hero! I've got to get back 'round to my own house on South Canal. You coming, Paddy?"

Paddy glanced at Russell, the old man's house, and then his friend, who shook his head, turned, and ran off. "In a minute! Let me give the codger one last chance to save himself."

Russell and Paddy kicked the door, but it didn't give. They went to the side of the house and smashed the window glass. There were curses from inside, and suddenly the kitten jumped through the shards and into the yard, then clawed its way up into the branches of a barren apple tree.

"Sir!" called Russell. "Let us in!"

"Go away!" The shutters inside the window were slammed shut and locked. Russell went to the other side of the house where the only other window was located, but that set of inside shutters had been locked, as well.

The grass in the old man's yard had broken into large patches of fire, and from over the roofs on the south side of the road, the approaching flames were taller now, closer, with the smoke rolling across the road in the wind like a mist. Russell covered his nose and drove his fist into the glass and the wood of the shutter. He saw the cut on his knuckles but didn't feel it. "You're going to die, sir!"

"I've got an axe and I'll chop you to pieces if you don't leave me be!" came the cry from inside.

"Either he will kill us or the fire will!" shouted Paddy over the growing sound of the wind and oncoming blaze. "We have to get out of here!"

"Sir!" Russell screamed a last time, but the old man wouldn't answer. Paddy was right, and Russell felt sickened at the knowledge. He ran to the apple tree, scooped up the trembling kitten and buttoned it inside his shirt with the tiny yellow head peeking out. The kitten mewled and tried to scratch, but couldn't get free.

They made it to the end of the block then down another, dodging a steam engine with its hoses and clanging bell and screaming drivers as it dashed down the middle of the street. The only thing Russell and Paddy could do was to get out of the way. The fire was winning its race.

They reached the tracks of the Galena and Chicago Railroads next to the river off Harrison Street and stopped, bending over to catch their breath. At the moment, they were out of harm's way. A cluster of frightened West Side citizens had also come to the tracks. They were coughing, crying, holding each other, and praying. A few had suitcases. Most, it seemed, had not had time to pack. One boy of about thirteen held tightly to a rope to which was tied a mangy, cream-colored dog. The dog saw the kitten and began to bark.

Russell rubbed the top of the kitten's head, trying to calm it. He couldn't stop thinking about the old man locked in his house. His mind played and replayed the imagine of the flames crossing the road, consuming the cottage. He could see the man cowering behind his bed, realizing that it was too late, that he was going to die. Russell dropped down onto the tracks, his head spinning. *God, bring a miracle to that poor old man, or let him perish quickly without pain and realization!* He could taste the soot in his mouth and smell the ash in his nostrils. Around him, the chatter was frightened but laced with a cautious hope.

"There's lots of fire engines out by now," came a young woman's voice. "They may stop the fire before it gets to my house. I live down on Ellsworth."

"The worst will be over soon," said a middle-aged man.

The talk went on and on, for a long time, becoming just a buzzing of noise in Russell's ears, none of it clear or intelligible.

But then Paddy shouted, "Look, it's shifted! It's coming this way!" The crowd turned to stare, and they were frozen for a moment in horror.

"We've to go back south," yelled another man, "or try to make the Van Buren Street Bridge."

"No!" said Paddy, pointing. "There are new flames there, too! We must cross the river here!"

People cried, "I can't swim!" "We're doomed!"

There were scattered, discarded beams and logs by the tracks, and Russell picked up a heavy plank and dragged it across to the edge of the river. The bank was steep, but not long. "You who can't swim," he said. "Take these in the water! Hold on for your lives, and you will float and survive! Don't be afraid!"

"But the babies?" said one mother with an infant in her arms and a toddler holding her hand.

"You need free hands for the boy," said Russell. "Put the baby in your blouse, like this cat! Don't be modest, there is no time!" The woman unbuttoned her blouse and slipped the baby inside, then buttoned it up again and tied it tightly closed with her shawl. The baby's eyes peeked out, wide and dark.

The people dragged the wood to the bank and slid down with them into the water. There were screams of fear and calls of encouragement all around. Paddy and Russell were the last to go, slipping the along the weeds into the cold water, holding separate ends of a broken railroad tie. The kitten mewled and scratched Russell's chest, trying to free itself from the shirt.

They paddled to the other side of the river behind the others on their floats, fighting the current with desperate arms and legs. A barge carrying grain nearly side-swiped them, but they kicked hard and made it past just in time. The boat crew saw all the people in the water, and shouted for them to be careful.

On the eastern bank, Russell clawed his way to the top of the retaining wall with the others. He clasped Paddy's hand and said, "You're a good man, Paddy. God bless you. Now there is someone I have to find before it's too late. If the fire leaps the river, she's in danger, and I can't let that happen!"

He made his way to Market Street, which led north, and as soon as he caught his breath, began to run in his soggy coat, the frightened kitten bouncing and hissing.

16

She fought with her arms and legs, pushing against the water and the slime at the bottom of the river, holding her breath even as her lungs demanded she open her mouth and breathe. She could hear nothing but the hissing of her own blood in her ears. *I can't escape a fire only to drown in this hellish river!*

One foot found a solid spot on the bottom, and with all her strength, she pushed with it and felt herself moving upward. Her arms battled the river, her teeth were clenched to keep from drawing in water. Her skirt tangled around her but she spun, throwing it loose. Her lungs burned with urgency, insisting that she breathe, *breathe!*

And then her head broke the surface and she gasped, fresh air flooding her lungs and making her feel faint. *I made it! Yes!* But then the weight of her clothes pulled at her again, and she began to sink. "No!" she screamed as her head was sucked under. Her arms fought, but did not hold her up. The world was drawn upward and away again.

Her thrashing hand struck something hard and cylindrical, and instinctively she grabbed it. She clung as tightly as she could, needing again to have a breath, aching to have a breath, fighting to crawl up, but she couldn't, her skirt was wrapped again and wouldn't shake free.

I have to breathe!

And the thing she was clutching began to move upward, dragging her with it. Again, her head broke the surface, and she gulped the air. Her eyes were filmy and she could only see hazy lights around her, and she could hear voices nearby.

"Grab her arms! Get her out, before she's gone!"

Katina was hoisted up and onto a solid surface, and she lay there panting, digging at her eyes to see.

"Miss, are you all right?" came a deep voice.

Katina tried her voice, and it was raspy and faint. "I don't know. Where am I? Who are you?"

"Martin Moberg, crew of the *Lady L*," said the voice. "Heading out to the lake before we catch fire! Saw you strike the water before our very eyes, knocked off the bridge you were, and we fished you out with a pole."

Katina forced herself to sit up. Beside her were two sailors, and all around the deck were barrels and bundles. Her head rolled, and she put her hand to her eyes. "We're going out to the lake?"

"Best place for now! The fire's just jumped the river south of here, and the wind is fierce with no sign of letting up. The lake will be safest."

"Safest," said Katina. She bent over and coughed onto the deck. "Yes, safest. That is best."

"Don't know how far the blaze will go," said the sailor. He was young and dark, with wind-chapped skin. He wore a white hat with a black band. "But we ain't waitin' round to see. It's going to be every man for himself tonight!"

Every man for himself. Katina rubbed her eyes and they at last came into focus. The boat was moving ahead steadily, with the Madison Street bridge behind them and the Randolph Street Bridge straight ahead. Just past that the river turned sharply to the right and, joined with the water from the North Branch, flowed through the main part of the city and into Lake Michigan.

Every man for….

"No, let me out, please!" she said. "There are people I care about, I can't leave them alone!"

The sailor laughed in disbelief. "Miss, do you hear yourself? What can you do against the fire?"

"I can do what I can do!"

"Miss?"

Katina got to her feet. They were moving under the Randolph Street Bridge. A crowd of spectators lined that bridge as they had the Madison Street Bridge.

Katina's head was aching and her ears still humming from

the fall into the water, but her voice was strong. "Let me off this boat!"

"We can't!"

The boat emerged from beneath the bridge and was steered toward the wider mouth of the Chicago River. As it took the turn, it came close to the log-reinforced plank wall on the river bank, and Katina pulled herself up onto several bundles at the edge of the boat's deck and stood, the wind whipping her face. Her soaked skirt hugged her legs. The wall was at least five feet from the boat. *Can I make it?*

"No!" cried Martin. The sailor came up behind her, and reached for her arm just as she dove off the boat, her hands outstretched. She slammed into the wall and slid downward, but her shoes dug as hard as they could into the wood, and her fingers clutched the splintery surface. She stopped sliding, and began climbing upward. Behind her, she could hear the sailor shout, "Good luck, little lady! You're a mad one at that, but good luck!"

Godspeed, Martin Moberg!

With every fiber of strength, Katina pulled herself to the top of the wall. Her wet clothes were heavy and the muscles in her right leg locked into a cramp. She muffled a cry, and forced herself up and over, where she dropped, rolled to her side, and drew her leg up to massage the painful knot.

She squinted at the sky. There were still stars visible amid thin ribbons of smoke. She couldn't cross the river to find Russell, so she would go back to Homeplace. *No, Homeplace is destroyed, burned to ashes last night by John Brandermill.* She would return to the Stick. The fire would be stopped, certainly, before it got that far. She would wait for Russell there. He would know to look for her at the Stick.

If he's alive, she thought.

"He is, and don't ever think that again!" she scolded herself. With that, she pushed herself to her feet against the pain in her leg.

She found herself in the yard of a single-story warehouse with boarded up windows surrounded on three sides with a tall, solid plank fence. Her heart pounded in her ears and the sound of the fire-alarm bells made her feel unsteady on her feet. *I'm going to faint,* she thought. *I've never fainted before, I wonder what it feels like....*

But something deeper inside her mind said, *Katina! Don't you dare give in now! Get out of that place!*

With that, she went about finding a way out of the warehouse yard. The gate was locked. There were barrels and crates by the short wharf on the riverside, but the barrels were too heavy to push over to roll, and the crates were impossible to lift. And so, she crouched down and began to push. With her jaw set and her shoulders tight, she pushed and huffed until the first of the crates had furrowed a path across the warehouse yard to the fence. It would take another two to make a step tall enough to climb over. She pushed a second crate over but could not lift it on top of the first. She dug her fingers under the edge and screamed with the effort, but neither will nor noise made it go up more than several inches before dropping back to the ground.

She clenched her fists. "I've got to get out!"

One of the warehouse windows had been poorly boarded, with a good seven inches of glass showing at the bottom. Katina lifted her skirt, wrapped her hand, and smashed in the glass. She shook the shards from her skirt then pulled herself up to stand in the sill. Once she'd gained her balance, she climbed onto the shingled roof. Then, standing precariously on the sloped surface, she edged around to the other side of the building, where the fence was close enough to straddle. On the other side of the fence was a straw-lined wagon which was likely used to carry crates of fragile items to the warehouse. The wagon was empty except for the straw, and Katina was thankful for the bit of luck. She eased her legs over the side of the fence and dropped into the straw. A new firebrand of pain shot up through the cramped muscle of her leg, but she sat still for a moment, massaging the knot. Then she got out of the wagon and down to the street.

On the river side of Market Street were huge wooden grain elevators, warehouses, smoke-stacked factories, and office buildings. Businesses, hotels, and nicer apartments, also made of wood, lined the other side. Tonight, the street was buzzing with people, awake with the increasingly insistent fire alarms, swarming toward the bridges to see the blaze. Katina watched them as she stood, holding on to the wagon and catching her breath. She realized suddenly how tired she was and wondered if she had the strength to make it to Quincy Street.

I have to get back there, she told herself, biting her lip to keep the tears from coming. Several carriages rattled by, and she could see the occupants, staring out the windows for a glimpse of the fire. If only they would offer her a ride. But, of course, they would not.

She began to walk, counting her steps to take her mind off how weak she felt. *I can't give in to this,* she insisted to her shaking body. *I'm strong. I can make it.*

She stayed out of the way of the curious crowd, clinging to the sides of the buildings and rubbing her eyes to keep the world in focus. Above the tall hotels and banks, she could see the sky growing brighter, obscuring the stars, as if the sun were rising in the southwest. She crossed the intersection of Washington Street and then Madison, where half a block to the right the two sets of crowds ran head-on into each other—those escaping across the bridge from the west and those still coming in to have a look. She counted her breaths as well as her steps now. Her mouth tasted of bile and the river water she had swallowed.

Three more blocks, she thought. *I'll get there.*

She could see that the flames were close, perhaps one block south of Quincy now, having been blown up the east side of the river.

God help us!

At the corner of Quincy and Market Street, there was nothing but bedlam. People who had been caught unaware, sleeping in their flats, were making a scramble to save some of their possessions before the wall of fire leapt into their street. There was a rain of sheets, pillows, coats, books, showering down to the road from second-, third-, and fourth-floor windows. Some people were already evacuating; others stood in the street, clutching what they could, crying out for family members who were not visible in the crowd. Thieves from Conley's Patch were helping themselves to items left unattended on the street, scooping up all they could hold and laughing. An old woman's soup cart was overturned and smashed in front of a wagon, and a man and woman in the wagon were screaming at the old woman. The horse at harness was snorting, the old woman was crying, the passengers kept yelling, and all Katina could think was, *Poor old lady, it wasn't her fault, whatever happened! Leave her alone!*

She didn't mean it!

Leave her alone!

The smoke was thick. Overhead, loose and flaming shingles arced above the rooftops and landed on the sidewalk by Katina. It was here. There was nothing to stop the fire now. If felt as if the earth beneath Katina's feet began to shake. Like a mountain crumbling into the sea. Like a Georgian house giving up its ghost to the torches of maniacal renegades.

I didn't mean it. Mother, Katherine, it wasn't my fault, I didn't mean it, Russell I didn't mean it!

And then the earth buckled one last time, and Katina dropped to the road in a dead faint.

17

Russell had reached Quincy Street well ahead of the fire and had gone directly to the Stick to find Katina. He was soaked to the skin and covered with thick and sticky soot, but the way he looked meant nothing. Finding her meant everything.

I cannot wait to hold her! he had thought. *To touch her and tell her how much I love her!*

But Alice had met him inside the Stick, where customers who had grown bored with the fire across the river had come to resume their drinking, cigar smoking, and merrymaking. She had told him that she had no idea where Katina was, but the expression on her face told Russell something was wrong.

Russell wriggled the panicked kitten out from his shirt and put it on the floor, where it staggered, shook itself off, and began to prowl the shadows beneath a nearby table and bat at dust balls. Alice said, "How precious! Did you save that little thing?"

But Russell took her by the shoulder and looked sternly into her eyes. "Are you sure you don't know where Katina is? She might be in her attic room, away from the noise."

"She isn't there, I know it," said Alice. The girl's lips rolled in between her teeth nervously. "She went with me out to the bridge to watch the fire but she didn't come back. She said she wanted to cross over to the West Side."

"Why would she do that?"

"She wanted to look for you. She knew your parents lived on De Koven, and she—"

"What?"

"She said she had to find you, no matter what."

Russell's heart sank. He shook his head, as if denying it would make it untrue. "That's impossible!"

"It's true, but maybe she's all right. She's smart, smarter

than me, for sure. She ain't gonna run smack headlong into a fire. You know she's scared of fires."

Russell let go of Alice and went to the open door to stare out at the citizens of Quincy Street, who had taken up vigil in the road, no longer staring at the inferno from the riverside but now waiting to see if their own homes and shops would be in peril. A few had brought out some bundles, but most were empty-handed. Ladies were huddled together, speaking to one another with grim faces; men were cross-armed and frowning, glancing around and up at the sky. An old soup-seller had found an opportunity and was wheeling her cart among the people, offering cuts of steaming pepper soup for three pennies a serving.

Someone touched Russell's arm. It was Madame Jocelyn, holding a cup of tea. "You look a fright, son," she said. "Like somebody dipped you in grease and rolled you in the hearth."

Russell took the cup but his hands shook so much he couldn't drink it. He put the cup down on the corner of a table. "I have to find her," he said.

Madame Jocelyn pointed her wrinkled finger at his face. "Now you talkin' stupid, mister. How many thousands of people in Chicago? How many thousands over on the West Side? Sit down, how something stronger than that blasted tea, and ease your worries. Alice, get us a couple brandies."

"Ma'am," said Russell. "you know I'm not one to give up, ever, when something is important."

Madame Jocelyn's nose twitched. "And you're a lunatic! You won't make it back across that river now, not for the love of God nor money. And if you did, you'd be burned up in your tracks. What good is that?"

At the piano, the tuned changed from a light, plinky ditty to a slow and somber hymn. One drunk at the bar turned on his seat, raised his glass, and said, "This is for them poor unfortunates on the other side of the river what is burned up in Hell's fire. May God keep their souls safe and keep us safe from that same fire!"

"Here, here!" said another man.

"To the dead and the living," said the girl at the piano. There was a second of silence as everyone in the saloon took a long swing from their glasses, jars, and bottles, and then the laughter and shouts began again.

Katina, Russell thought, his fingers taking hold of the door frame and squeezing so hard that splinters were driven into his skin. *Please, wherever you are, be alive!*

Alice brought two glasses half-filled with dark liquid, and Madame Jocelyn took one while Alice held the tray with the other toward Russell. He looked at it and said, "No, thank you."

"C'mon, you old starched-britches," said Madame Jocelyn with an attempt at a smile. "It'll take the sting off o' life. You'll feel better."

Russell's arm shot out and knocked the glass from the tray. "I don't want to feel better! I want to find Katina!"

With that, he darted out to the street and into the milling mob.

A fire engine raced past on Quincy and then turned south of Fifth Avenue, spraying rocks and dirt from the dry road surface. People jumped out of the way. Beside and behind the smoking contraption ran more firefighters, their faces tight with determination, their arms swinging in militaristic unison.

"Fire's just four blocks away now!" cried one fireman through his horn. "On our side of the river, coming on the wind! Be prepared!"

The crowd began anxiously looked up at the sky. The smoke was growing thicker, darker. Several large smoldering chunks of debris drifted from over the buildings and down to the street at their feet. It was then that the people saw and understood the truth. Their street was going to burn, and soon.

While Russell stamped on the flaming chunks that had struck the road, other folks scattered like dust in the wind, making for their shacks, their tenements, their apartments, and their gambling halls and shops, to collect what they could. Another fire engine rattled past and Russell knew he had to make a decision.

I must stay here and help these people get out safely, he thought. *Or I must look for Katina.* The choice cut his heart like a razor. How could he choose? It was as if he were being asked which leg he preferred to have amputated, his right or his left.

Across the street from the Stick, upstairs apartment windows were slammed open and people began throwing things down to the road. Buckets, blankets, dolls, baskets, tools. Anything that wouldn't break came tumbling down, and some things that did break. More embers and ash blew overhead and landed on Quincy Street rooftops, none of them large enough to set the roofs on fire, but a foreshadowing of what was to come. People who had been sleeping through the ordeal were now awakening, gazing from their windows and rubbing their eyes, and then screaming at the realization of what was happening.

Family wagons, driven by fathers or sons and hitched to horses from nearby stables, pulled up in front of the tenements on both sides of the street and braked. Horses danced nervously in place as the families threw crates, mattresses, and other bundles into the wagons, and then scooped up from the road the items they'd thrown down. People who had no wagons stuffed things under their arms and headed off quickly. Bandits emerged from the dark underground rooms of Conley's Patch and took advantage of the confusion to steal what they could.

With dismay, Russell saw Bruce Charles darting back and forth, stuffing his pockets full of forks and spoons and odd, broken trinkets from the road dust.

"Bruce!" he shouted at the boy then ran over and grabbed him by the arm. He turned the boy's coat pockets inside out, dumping the contents. "What are you doing? You're stealing!"

Bruce yanked his arm away from Russell, his face contorted with shame and denial. "But they don't need these! It's only spoons and such. They'd be stamped to bits on the road."

"It's wrong to steal."

"I'm not stealing! I'm helping myself! Nobody's gonna miss these things!"

"Will you never learn?" Russell shouted. "Will nothing ever change? I've accomplished nothing. I've wasted my time!"

Bruce spun away.

"Bruce, come back!"

But the boy was gone, vanished in the crowd.

This is my answer, he thought, heartsick. *What I've done here has been a waste of time. But I will find Katina! God, let her be alive, and if not, let me die in my effort, for living would be unbearable!*

He forced his way against the crowd, imagining the difficulty he would find trying to cross the bridge to the West Side. He would fight if he had to in order to get through. He would go all the way back to De Koven, every fiery step of the way.

There was an old woman crying in the middle of the street. It was the soup-seller. The terrified woman had her hands cupped over her ears. *I can't stop for her, I haven't time!* Russell thought, but he knew he had to, even if for just a moment.

"Ma'am, where do you live?" he asked. "The fire's coming and you can't stay here!"

"I don't have a home!"

"Where do you sleep?"

"In the tunnels beneath Billy Spilman's dance hall. I cook in the alley."

"You need to get north, and quickly!"

"My cart's stuck in a rut in this bloody road and I can't move it!"

"Let me help you move it. It's your livelihood and you won't want to lose it."

But before Russell could rock the cart wheel out of the hole, a wagon bearing a family and its belongings came barreling down Quincy, straight at them. Russell leapt out of the way, dragging the old woman with him. The horse pulling the wagon whinnied and tried to jump over the soup cart. Its hind legs came down on the cart, smashing it to bits, and the front right wheel of the wagon struck the cart and shattered.

The man in the wagon jumped out and threw his hands up in the air. The woman in the wagon pointed a threatening finger at the old woman and cursed her at the top of her lungs. "Look what you've done, you damned witch!" The children in the wagon began to wail.

Russell took hold of the horse's reins and urged it forward, freeing its legs from the wreckage. The man yelled at Russell, at the old woman, at his wife.

"We're doom with a broken wheel!" he said. "We're

destroyed! How will we ever escape now?"

Several flaming cinders fell to the road beside Russell and the horse. There was no time to argue.

"You'll have to carry what you can!" said Russell. "The children can ride the horse and you lead."

The man continued to complain, the old woman and the children continued to cry, and Russell thought, *This delay may cost me Katina! Why did I even bother to stop?*

And then he saw her, half a block away, staring straight ahead as if in a trance. Her clothes were wet, her body quivering. He blinked, certain he was dreaming.

But he was not.

Katina!

Her eyes rolled up in her head and she dropped to the road amid the pounding of feet and hooves and wagon wheels.

18

Russell carried Katina inside the Stick, where some of the evening patrons were still at the bar, draining their glasses of whiskey, and others were at table, dealing out cards as if nothing was going on outside. Madame Jocelyn was on a chair at a corner table, puffing on a pipe and dangling a string for the little yellow kitten to catch. Alice paced back and forth near the door, and she gasped when Russell came in and laid Katina on the bar.

"You found her!" Alice cried. "And she's dead!"

"No," said Russell. "She's alive, only overcome. I need to revive her and then we all need to get out of here immediately. The rooftops all along Quincy are starting to smolder!"

Alice patted Katina's face tentatively but Russell pushed her aside and shook Katina firmly. "Katina! You must wake up!" And to Madame Jocelyn he called, "Ma'am! You have to evacuate right now! There's no hope anything will be spared, and the fire is breathing down our necks like the hounds of hell!"

But the old woman only took her pipe out from between her teeth and said, "It won't burn the Stick. Nothing dares to confront me. You know my reputation."

"Stubbornness won't keep the flames asway!" Russell said. "An old man perished in his cottage today for worthless contempt and hardheadedness! Do what I say! Alice, there's but a moment. If there is anything you need, get it now or never!"

Most of the men, drunk as they were, seemed to catch Russell's urgency. They wrapped their arms about each other's shoulders and stumbled for the door. Only three at the gambling table waved Russell off with a flick of their hands. One said, "Got a bet going here. If I win, the wind's gonna shift and go back where it came from." His gambling partners howled with laughter.

Alice ran up the steps behind the piano. Madame Jocelyn continued to smoke her pipe and play with the kitten.

"Katina," said Russell, fanning his hand. "Wake up. I have no wagon to put you in and we'd do so much better if you were awake."

Katina groaned slightly.

"Wake up!"

Slowly, Katina's eyes opened, unfocused at first then steadying and locking squarely on Russell's face.

"Oh," she managed. "Russell, it's you?"

Russell nodded.

"Truly?"

"Yes, dearest. And we've got to be moving."

"The fire!" Katina gasped. "The fire! Did you see the fire coming?"

"Yes, but we'll get out. It's starting to catch along the street and we can't waste any time. Can you walk?"

Holding Katina around her waist, Russell lifted her to her feet. She grimaced as if her leg hurt but said nothing. "I can walk," she said. "Russell, I can't believe you are here. I will wake up any moment and be back, trapped in the warehouse yard!"

"You're soaked."

"And so are you."

"I've been in the river."

"And so have I!"

"I hated being in the river."

"So did I," she said, smiling at last. The smile was the most beautiful thing Russell had seen in his lifetime. Then her smile vanished and tears came into her eyes. She said, "I'm so sorry, Russell. I didn't trust you and I should have."

"I wasn't understanding, I wasn't patient," said Russell. He held Katina's face. "I was coming to find you. I resented an old woman and her cart in the road for slowing me down. But if it wasn't for that, I would not have stopped and I would not have seen you."

"Things sometimes happen for a reason," Katina said.

"I love you. And we have to go!"

Several dresses were tossed down the steps, and then a

brocade satchel, which landed squarely on the piano keys with a plunk. Then Alice could be heard up the stairs calling, "Becky's up here! And I can't get her out! She's too sick and too heavy!"

Through the open front door blew a billow of smoke. Russell glanced outside. The roof of the tenement directly across the street had caught fire. Some of the upstairs windows belched flames, and from the other upstairs windows, tenants screamed that the stairs were on fire and there was no way down but to jump.

"We must get Becky!" cried Katina.

This broke Madame Jocelyn's spell. She dropped her pipe to the tabletop and scooped up the kitten, who uttered a startled meow. She snatched Katina's satchel from the piano keys, put the kitten inside, and buckled up all but the third buckle so to leave an airhole. "Get out, boys!" she said to the gamblers, but the men at the table glowered and sat tight, holding their cards as if daring anyone to make them move.

Russell darted for the steps and Katina tried to follow, but still seemed weak, for she grabbed onto the edge of a table and stopped, leaning over. "Get outside with Madame Jocelyn," Russell shouted. "And head down into Rat's Alley. I don't think the worst of the fire's there yet. Alice and I'll get Becky and meet you there!"

"But Russell—" began Katina, but Madame Jocelyn took her arm and said, "He's right, girl. We got to move!"

They hurried out the door, Katina's satchel on Madame Jocelyn's right elbow, Katina on her left.

Russell raced up the stairs to the second floor. Alice was inside the third bedroom, standing beside Becky's simple iron bed, one hand over her mouth, staring at the window. The glass had been broken from flying debris and the windowsill had caught fire. "We're going up!" Alice shrieked. "The Stick's burning!"

Becky was sitting up in bed, teetering back and forth. Her red hair was loose and stringy, hanging down her nightgown. "I'm sick," she said simply. "I can't run."

"Hold on to us," said Alice. She bent down and Becky grasped her neck. Russell slid his arm around Becky's waist.

She was hot with fever and moving her was going to be difficult.

But we have to try!

The curtains in the windows went up in a flash and the fire reached around to the wall, igniting the dirty flowered wallpaper with a crackle and sizzle.

Holding Becky as tightly as possible, they walked her out the door and eased her toward the steps. Russell knew things were going from bad to worse when he saw the smoke in the stairwell, rolling up from the first floor. Then came shouts of the cardplayers, and Alice cried out, "Fire's downstairs, too! We're done for!"

The scene at the bottom of the staircase confirmed their worst fears. The flames had blown across the street and had set the left side of the door frame ablaze. Cinders had landed inside on the threadbare runner and it was smoldering.

The three gamblers were staring, having finally dropped their cards in a flutter across the table and floor. One held his bowler hat to his chest as if out of some horrified respect for the inferno. "I've died and gone to hell!" he said, his voice slurring. "Looka this, Morgan, we gonna meet the devil together!"

"Bring him on, the butcher!" said the inebriated Morgan. "Always meant to face him head-on!"

"I ain' givin' up, not yet!" said the third man. He grabbed up an open decanter of whiskey, took a swig, and said, "And this is comin' with me, sirs!"

Russell and Alice reached the first floor, holding Becky. There was no back exit to the saloon; Madame Jocelyn always feared burglars sneaking in so this was the only way out. The three gamblers pushed past Russell and Alice and made it to the front door. They stumbled through, skirting the burning door frame. Alice and Russell followed with Becky, out to the street.

Russell's face and arms were struck with nearly intolerable heat. He could barely believe what he was seeing. The flames across the street reached up from the buildings and clawed at the sky like talons. Wagons left unattended along the road were beginning to smoke, as were crates and bundles dropped by those who had escaped. People still ran in the streets, confused and terrified, attempting to carry whatever of value they could handle amid the fiery rain, crazed by the scorching heat. A fire engine, hooked into the hydrant near the corner, had its canvas hose and powerful stream of water aimed at the tenement directly across from the Stick. The tenement was engulfed but not empty, and a hysterical woman was leaning out a fifth-floor window.

"She's going to jump!" said Alice.

"God help me!" the woman cried. She swung her legs out the window as red tongues of fire lapped out after her, and she paused only a second before letting go and plummeting to the street. She fell hard, her head hitting the edge of a wagon, and collapsed in a heap. Silent. Motionless.

"This ain't happening!" screamed Alice.

Embers filled the air, raining down upon them. Russell and Alice held Becky up and headed north for Rat's Alley with the gamblers close behind, cursing each time a cinder landed on their heads. The man with the whiskey took a quick sip then cradled the decanter in his arm as if it were a baby.

By now, Rat's Alley might be burning, Russell thought. But the alley cut over to Adams, and then another alley cut over to Monroe and then Madison. *If we stay this course, we will end up on Franklin Street, and then it will be just a short distance to a bridge that crosses the Chicago River to North Division where, God willing, the fire will not follow!*

They reached the entrance to Rat's Alley. The roofs of some of the buildings at the entrance had begun to burn but those farther in appeared unaffected. People who lived in the rooms along the alley were yelling and throwing items out of windows—stools, dishes, boxes, clothing, lanterns, and anything else they thought they could save. Shattered items lay in heaps.

As Russell and the others darted into the alley, several burning shingles from the roof of the rattletrap bakery on the corner blew off and down. Russell was struck on the back but he quickly shook it off. One of the gamblers was hit by a shingle that set his trouser leg on fire, but he tore the trousers off, threw them aside, and caught up to the other in his long johns.

They hurried on, dodging things hurled from above and the frantic people in the alley who were reaching upward, trying to catch what they could.

Then Alice shouted, "Becky's ablaze!"

Becky, who had been trying her best to keep her feet moving between Russell and Alice, was so dazed that she was unaware that a large, red-hot ember had landed in the back of her hair and set it on fire.

Alice let go of Becky and slapped her friend's hair with her hands. The fire raced upward to Becky's scalp. Alice screamed. Russell reached down to grab a handful of dirt from the alley to throw on Becky's head to put out the flame. But in that moment, Becky realized in that she was burning. She took off in a mad run, stumbling over the broken items littering the ground. People squealed at the sight and jumped out of her way. Then Becky tripped and fell into a pile of blankets. In that instant, someone threw a kerosene lantern from a second floor window. It struck Becky on the back and shattered, coating the young woman in kerosene. Her entire body was engulfed in fire.

Becky's screams turned into a demon's shriek. She covered her head with her hands and writhed on the ground. Russell chased after her, dropped to his knees and rolled her over and over in the blanket, trying to smother the fire. But the blanket caught fire around her. Russell could see Becky's open eyes, staring helplessly out through the flames.

Alice put her hands over her ears.

Russell threw more dirt on Becky and beat at the flames. But it was too late. The fire was too great. After agonizing moments, Becky shuddered, spasmed, and then went limp. She was gone. Alice turned away and wept. The gamblers stared, their eyes huge and horrified. Ash and household items continued to rain down around them.

Russell fell back onto his knees, held his hands to the sky, and screamed, "I don't understand! Let me understand these terrible things!" *Why? Why?!*

There was no answer.

Russell finally extinguished the flame and then, as gently and quickly as possible, he moved Becky to the side of the alley.

He tried to cover her body with one of the remaining blankets but a man yelled at him to leave his belongings alone. Russell offered a quiet prayer that Becky was now at peace. The others whispered, "Amen." There was nothing more to be done.

The group continued up the alley until they reached the ruins of the old garment factory. There they found Madame Jocelyn and Katina in the shadows, hiding and waiting. The wind had not yet brought the fire this far along the alley, but it was obvious it wouldn't be long.

When Katina saw Russell, she fell into his arms. "Thank you!" she said, her breath soft on his neck, soothing the singed flesh. "Thank you for coming and finding us! With you, I know we'll be safe!"

Russell kissed her check but could not speak of Becky. Some things were too terrible on the tongue. Alice and the gamblers said nothing either, but it was only moments before Madame Jocelyn asked, "And where's our sweet Miss Becky?"

Alice shook her head. It was enough.

Madame Jocelyn made a hardened sound in her throat, and Katina said, "God rest her soul."

It was all they could offer in her memory, because the fire behind them was not slowing down and the sound of sirens continued to grow louder on the blistering evening wind.

19

"We'll make it to north stretch of river," shouted Russell as they stepped from the ruins of the factory and back into the alley. The inferno was not far behind them now, moving up Rat's Alley, setting fire to buildings on both sides. The blaze crackled and popped and the heat in the alley was intense. Katina opened her satchel to make sure the kitten was still safe. Its yellow head peeked out and it hissed, angry at its confinement. She quickly closed the satchel back up. Madame Jocelyn, who somewhere along the way had lost a shoe, gazed down at her bare toes as if she'd never seen them before.

"The fire will be under control before it gets to North Division, I'm sure," Russell said as they began moving again, picking their pace up to keep ahead of the fire. "Those rich folks over there wouldn't stand for it!"

Katina nodded, knowing how hard he was trying to give them hope. She ran along beside him. Her leg still ached, but not as badly.

"But I need to stop at an abandoned house in the alley off Adams Street," Russell continued. "Bruce lives in the tunnel underneath. If he's there I want him to come with us."

Katina nodded again. She thought she knew the house he was speaking of, a crumbling two-story structure several blocks ahead.

The exhausted crew moved quickly along the alley, Russell, Alice, Katina, in front, Madame Jocelyn following, and the gamblers huffing and groaning and bringing up the rear. They passed a decaying tenement, an old stable, a crumbling shed. And there was Brandermill's boarding house. Katina glanced over at, remembering her old life.

It seems long ago. Like another lifetime. I can barely recall...

Then the boardinghouse door slammed open and two men stalked out. Katina gasped. One man was thin and clean-shaven. The other was older, with a bristly beard and thick brows.

John Brandermill!

"Well!" cried John Brandermill from the boarding house stoop. "Look who we run into during a fire, Ardie! If it isn't the man who turned me in for killing Meg!"

Russell did not acknowledge the men. The group kept moving. Suddenly there was a gunshot, and a bullet bit the ground in front of Russell's feet. The group flinched and whirled around. Both men on the stoop were pointing pistols at Russell. "I know it's you," said John. "You look just like what they's said, and you's with these people they say you spend time with. Them wenches, that short little gal. I thought I'd burned you up in the butcher shop, but you's a tough old hide, ain't you?"

John and Ardie stepped down off the stoop, the guns still trained on Russell. "Gonna kill you, know that?" John grinned darkly.

"Let these others go," said Russell. The calm in his voice surprised Katina.

"Others? Oh, look, Ardie, we have a man in his undergarments!" The two laughed darkly.

"I said, let these others go," repeated Russell.

"Sure," said John. "The rest of you is free to leave. Now leave!"

The gamblers took the cue to heart. They were off in a spray of dirt. But Madame Jocelyn, Alice, and Katina stood their ground.

This isn't happening! Katina thought. *This is a nightmare within a nightmare!*

Holding their pistols steady, the two men stopped just eight feet in front of Russell. John shook his head and grinned. "My building'll be burning in a few minutes. Wind's bringing that damned fire and we can't stop it. And look there, see? That old tenement down there's just catchin' fire. Ain' long 'til it's here. No worries. I ain' got no boarders no more. I closed the boarding house when I got out of jail. Didn' want to see their pitiful faces anymore, lookin' at me like I killed my wife. Been livin' alone in there and I like it."

"Hurry," said Russell. "Leave your guns, please, and come with us and save yourselves."

"Ha!" said John. His beard twitched. "I don't think so. I don' like you, Russell Cosgrove."

"You don't have to like me," Russell began. "Just—"

Ardie's pistol went off. The bullet whizzed past Russell's ear. Katina gasped and grabbed Russell's arm. Ardie laughed.

"Flame or gunshot?" asked John. "Which way you wanna die, Mr. Cosgrove? Lock you up in one of my closets and let the fire take you, or I can shoot you here. What'll it be?"

"Leave him alone!" demanded Katina.

"Want to die with him, lady?" asked Ardie.

"Katina," said Russell, pulling her hand from his arm and pushing her away firmly. "It'll be all right."

"No, it won't!"

"Mr. Cosgrove, convince these ladies to move on or I'll shoot them first," said John.

"Katina, please go," Russell said. Then he gave her nod that said, *I'll be all right. I have a plan. Please go and I'll catch up to you!*

Her heart twisting with fear, Katina began to back away from Russell and the men with the pistols. Alice took her hand and squeezed it tightly.

Russell turned to face John. "If you must fight me, do it without the pistol. Like men, not boys."

"My pistol talks for me," said John.

"Real men fight without needing weapons," said Russell.

"I'll fight him, John," said Ardie. "I'd like to kill him with my bare hands, like I killed my brother. Snap! Broken neck."

John seemed to consider this. Katina stopped backing up. Alice and Madame Jocelyn hissed for her to keep moving but she couldn't.

"We may all die in the fire, anyway," Russell said. "Care to make a quick sport of it, a wager?"

"What kind of wager?"

"There's no time!" shouted Katina. "We have to go!"

"You're a gambling man," said Russell. "If I win fisticuffs

with Ardie, without so much as a scratch, you let me go. If Ardie cuts me, much less breaks my neck, I've lost. You can shoot me, lock me in a closet, your choice. Ardie will prove what kind of man he is this way."

This can't be happening, Katina thought. *This is wrong! Let this be a dream, a terrible dream!* The crackling and popping of the fire was even louder now; brilliant orange and yellow danced along the buildings not far away. The air was hotter and the smell of death and ash stronger and more bitter. Flaming matter landed on the roof of the boarding house and had begun to smolder.

"Let me fight him, John," said Ardie.

John shrugged. "Why not? But if you lose, Cosgrove, I just might go after and kill your women, too."

Russell didn't respond to this. With fists raised, he began skipping backward along the alley toward the now-burning tenement building. Ardie threw down his pistol and went after him.

"I'm a good fighter! I'll knock you on your face, you coward!"

Russell took a quick step toward Ardie, threw a jab, and then jumped back, his face flushed red with heat and determination. John Brandermill followed at a close distance, pointing his gun at Russell and chucking.

Russell's getting John's attention away from us, Katina thought. *He's giving us a chance to escape. But he's heading toward the worst of the fire! Why?!*

"Russell!" Katina shouted.

Madame Jocelyn said, "We have to go, Katina!"

"I can't leave him!"

"Go, Katina!" called Russell.

"No!" said Katina.

"Katina, we have to!" said Alice.

Suddenly Ardie lunged at Russell and grabbed him around the waist. They struck the graveled ground with an "ugh!" and rolled back and forth, Ardie trying to smash Russell's face but Russell managing to lean away in time. Then Russell broke free and leapt to his feet. He hopped back several yards, close—too close—to the burning tenement. "Come and get me, Ardie!"

Ardie charged, bellowing, and Russell jumped out of the

way in time to send Ardie in a stagger. Russell grabbed up a broken beam lying at the side of the alley and, gripping one end, swung it hard, aiming for Ardie's shoulders. He caught the man solidly in the back. Ardie croaked and fell to the ground.

"I won!" shouted Russell, spinning to face John. "Not a cut on me."

"But Ardie's not dead!" John yelled.

"I didn't say I'd kill him, just beat him."

"Get up, Ardie!" said John. "Don't lose my bet!"

"Get up, Ardie!" said Russell. "We have to get away, and now or we'll all die!"

Ardie groaned but didn't get up.

Thank God! Russell won the bet! Katina thought. She wanted to run to him but Madame Jocelyn pulled her back. "Let's *go*! I don't want to burn to death! Russell will join us!" the old woman yelled.

Russell grabbed Ardie's arm but the man lay, unable to move. "John, help me! We have to get him up! We have to go!"

John waved his pistol at Russell. "Kill him or I'll kill you!"

Russell dropped Ardie's arm. "No!"

"Do it!" demanded John.

And at that moment, with a deafening crack, the rotted, burning tenement gave way, the remainder of its roof falling in on itself and the outer wall falling with a roar and a fiery crash onto the alley and on top of Russell and Ardie.

"No!" Katina screamed. She struggled against Madame Jocelyn's and Alice's firm grips.

"Ha!" shouted John Brandermill, who had jumped back and barely missed being caught in the collapse. "Fire did it for me! Russell's dead, burned up and gone! And sorry, Ardie, but that's the way it goes sometimes." John turned and hurried from the burning remains. He called out to the women as he passed them, "Lost his bet, he did! Ha!" Manically laughing, he continued on out to Adams Street, and was gone.

Katina fell against Madame Jocelyn. "No, God, not this! Tell me Russell's alive!"

"Shhh, he's gone," said Madame Jocelyn. "There's no way he survived that. But we have to move on."

"Dear God, no! I can't go! I can't leave him!"

Alice wept soundlessly, holding Katina's hand. Katina head felt as if it were spinning in sickening circles.

"Now!" said Madame Jocelyn, shaking Katina soundly. "We must get to the river! He's gone, Honey. Listen to me! Listen! It ain't safe to stay here! Russell would want us to save ourselves." With that, Katina turned and went with Alice and Madame Jocelyn up the alley, heading north. She couldn't feel her feet beneath her, she could barely catch her breath. What had happened had happened and she couldn't turn back time. Tears as hard as rocks pressed the backs of her eyes and disbelief hot as fire seared her heart.

They reached Adams and crossed over into the alley on the other side. Madame Jocelyn was talking to her, the woman's red-painted mouth was moving, but Katina couldn't hear her words.

My love is dead! There is nothing worth anything, nothing worth living for! Is this destiny? Damn destiny!

They passed an empty two-story house with broken windows and a dilapidated porch, and a voice in Katina's mind said, *Stop.*

She stopped. She rubbed her eyes and frowned.

I can do what I can do.

Russell had said that many times.

"I can do what I can do," whispered Katina.

"What?" asked Madame Jocelyn, tugging Katina's arm. "Young lady, we have to keep going!"

"No, not yet."

"Why did you stop?" asked Alice.

"This place," she whispered.

"What about this place?"

"This is Bruce's hideout. Just as Russell described it. We have to see if the boy's here."

"Why?"

"Because it's what Russell wanted!" Katina felt rage at the question. "He wanted to get Bruce to safety!"

Madame Jocelyn frowned.

Kneeling down on the dirty, graveled alley, Katina peered

into the dark and cobwebby space beneath the house. "Bruce? Bruce Charles? Are you there?"

There was silence. Madame Jocelyn stomped her foot impatiently. "Enough Katina! He's not there. Let's go!"

"Bruce, it's Katina! Please come with us. It's too dangerous here. We're going to safety in North Division!"

A rat scurried out over her hand. She shook it off. "Bruce!"

And then a small voice from deep in the black shadows said, "I can't come with you."

"Why not?"

"I wasn't gonna do more bad things, like Russell taught me. But I did. I stole things people was tossin' in the road. Russell yelled at me. I don't want him to yell at me again."

Katina's heart clenched at the sound of Russell's name. "Come with me. We've all done bad things."

"Russell out there with you?"

"Not…not right now. Please come with us."

There was a pause then slowly, the boy appeared from the darkness, crawling on his hands and knees. Katina took his hand and helped him up. She brushed him off and gave him a quick, tight hug. He didn't pull away. "We've all done bad things," she repeated softly around the grief in her throat. "But we've all done good things, too, and we're going to survive this. Come with us."

He said nothing, but Katina could feel his head moving up and down. *Yes.*

Together they hurried north, closing the distance to the Chicago River.

There was a mob along the river's edge, shoulder to shoulder, and from where she stood on Franklin Street, Katina could see that all the bridges spanning the water to North District were swarming with frantic people, their wagons, crates, bundles, and animals. Babies cried in mothers' arms and fathers shoved to get their families through the mass of bodies. Mules were frozen in place on the river's edge, braying over the shouts and the wind, refusing to move. To the south, the fire was visible over the buildings of the business district, rushing northward in the wind. It could be just minutes before an arm of it reached the river to burn those who waited there and to jump the water to the North Side.

"We gotta cross!" yelled Alice. "We gotta get to a bridge!"

"We won't make it!" Katina shouted. Inside the satchel, the kitten struggled, sticking its nose out from beneath the flap but unable to escape. "People can barely move on the bridge. Look. They're piled atop each other!"

The river was crowded with boats making for Lake Michigan. Small boats skirted beneath the bridge but the tall ones were jammed up, waiting for the bridges to be turned in order to let them out. Several boats were burning and their crews had jumped into the river, clutching anything they could find that would float.

Katina pushed through the people, beckoning the others to follow. She found a pile of shattered furniture, destroyed when the owners had thrown it from an overhead apartment window. "We won't make the bridge! Get in the river with this!"

People near here stared as though she were crazy, but others saw the wisdom of her words, and, dropping what they were carrying, snatched up lengths of wood that had once been part of chairs, dressers, tables. Katina and Alice lifted the headboard that had broken off a mahogany bed, and Bruce and Madame Jocelyn each grabbed a bedpost.

At the river's edge, they watched as some brave people slipped down the retaining wall into the water.

Russell, Katina thought. *God bless you and keep you. Thank you for your love, courage, and compassion. May I carry on your legacy.*

She broke into sobs as she followed Alice, Madame Jocelyn, and Bruce into the river.

20

Russell was struck on the back by a burning plank and knocked down. He bucked violently, knocking the plank away. Red-hot wreckage was piled around him and over him, rippling and crawling with the heat as if a million glowing slugs clung to their surfaces. But none of the pile was directly on top of him, as some of the beams and planks had snagged on each other and were held at an angle three feet over his head, forming a small space in which he lay. Russell's clothes began to smoke.

Get out get out get out!

His foot was trapped beneath Ardie and he kicked at the man. Ardie was clearly dead, his torso crushed and his body on fire.

GET OUT!

Russell jerked his leg free and yanked his coat over his head as best he could. Then, without letting himself think about it because if he did, he would have hesitated, he shoved as hard as he could, rolling out of the space that protected him and through a solid wall of fire. It felt as though the skin on one side of his face was splitting in the heat. He screamed as one of his hands blistered. But suddenly, he realized he was clear of the collapsed building and out in the open.

He rolled over several more times with his face and hands tucked, clearing the burning rubble. The nerves of his burned hand and face felt as if he were being skinned alive, but he *was* alive.

He lay, panting in the dust of the alley. His ears rang and his heart pounded.

I'm alive!

And I have to get up! I have to get away from here or I'll surely be roasted!

Russell drew his knees up under him and forced himself to stand. He wobbled on his feet, the pain in his hand and face like razors cutting into his flesh. Smoke held heavy in the alley. Russell gagged and coughed, closing his eyes against the sting.

I can still stand.

He took several steps.

I can still walk.

And I have to find Katina!

He took several more steps then opened his eyes.

The people in the alley were gone. Some of the possessions thrown to the ground had been spirited away; much still lay in heaps. Most buildings' roofs were now on fire; some were burning in their entirety, with flames curling out through windows. Ash and embers rained down.

He couldn't go the same way Katina had gone. The collapsed tenement blocked the entire width of the alley. He'd have to go back to Quincy and make it north to the Chicago River some other way, where he prayed Katina and the other women had gone.

What if John Brandermill shot them?

Tears burned his eyes and rolled down his cheeks.

I can still cry.

He ran.

As fast as he could he raced down the alley, wincing with pain, thinking only of finding Katina and praying she was still alive, not knowing what he would do if she was not.

If Brandermill killed her, I'll swear I'll find and kill him! If the fire has killed her, there is nothing I can kill for retribution.

He reached the end of Rat's Alley and stumbled out onto Quincy.

"She must be alive!" he panted. He stopped and bent over to catch his breath. The world folded and rippled beneath his feet. Smoke and ash whirled like storm clouds.

"Hey, son!" The voice was of a man nearby. Russell looked up to see a grizzled fireman standing nearby, waving his arm.

Other firemen were scattered along the street, rolling up a charred hose onto the fire engine. There were puddles on the alley as well as sizzling rubble. Some of the men's uniforms were smoking from close contact with the intense heat. One man had thrown his broad-brimmed hat to the ground and it lay there, a blackened, scorched mess. Some buildings were merely smoking now. Others continued to burn down the length of the street.

The fireman trotted over to Russell and took his arm. "Son, we got to go."

He took Russell's arm but Russell pulled away. He had felt hopeless before, but never this utterly defeated. "We're all going to die, aren't we?" he muttered. "There's no hope, is there?"

The fireman took Russell's arm again. "Don't you say that! You're coming with me with me."

As the fire engine's horses stomped, impatient to be away from the terrible scene, and the fire leapt overhead, the fireman led Russell to the steam engine. There, he was hoisted up to stand between two firemen on the back runner. "Hold tight!" one man next to him shouted. "We're heading north!"

Russell grabbed the railing behind the boiler as tightly as he could with his good hand.

With a clanging and belching of steam, the engine clattered along Quincy Street to Market and turned north. Here, crowds of panicked people were also fleeing north. They shouted and shoved each other out of the way for the firemen.

The world is burning, Russell thought. *It's the end of everything.*

Russell the gripped the rail even more tightly as the engine swayed back and forth. He was in agony from the burns on his hand and face. Even his chest and legs had been singed through his clothing.

"You headin' for the river?" the fireman beside Russell yelled.

Russell nodded.

"Our hose got burned up, can't use it," shouted the fireman. "Our station's a block from the river and we got to get back there right away."

Russell nodded again. He locked his fingers and let hell

roll past. There was an explosion somewhere nearby, and the fireman said, "Gotta be the gasworks!"

The city's gone. It's an inferno that we cannot escape.

And the Russell glanced down from the engine, and in that passing instant he saw a young mother holding a toddler to her chest. The woman's face was locked in determination. She was ash-covered, her hair ragged and singed, and her dress ripped at the neck. She had nothing with her but her precious child. She was going north to the river and her expression told Russell that nothing would stop her.

She's not giving up.

She still has hope.

The fire engine roared on, pressing through the crowds.

I can't give up. Not yet.

I don't know what I'll find.

I don't know if I'll survive.

But I can't give up.

Katina may still be alive.

Dear God, let me find her!

Russell closed his eyes.

In what seemed like seconds, the fireman was nudging him. "Off you go, sir! This is Lake Street. Hop quick now, we've got to make a repair before we're at it again."

Russell opened his eyes. "Bless you," he said.

Gentlemen and ladies from the business section of town were on the street and sidewalks, looking much less elegant now. They wore the same fear in their eyes as any other person, rich or poor, and they pushed just as hard to get where they needed to go. Russell let the crowd usher him to the river's edge, where he stared at the broad spectrum of a city in torment. On his side of the wide Chicago River, people struggled with everything they could carry toward the bridges; on the other side, spectators stared back across the water, transfixed. In the river floated burning boats, dead bodies, and numerous living people clinging to scrap wood.

How could he find Katina in all this?

Let her be alive! Let her be safe!

"We're going to die, aren't we?" asked a gentleman next to Russell. He was well dressed, with a vest, pocket watch chain, and tailored linen jacket and trousers. He was leaning on a broken wooden door that he'd propped up beside himself. "I will die, I know it. I can't get to the bridge, and if I could, I couldn't make it across. Everything's burning behind and around us. The offices, the shops, the homes, even the blasted sidewalks, up in flames like paper a child has set ablaze for the fun of it. But I'll die right here by the river because I won't be able to cross over."

It hurt Russell to speak. "Because the bridge is too crowded?"

"No," said the man. "It's my leg. It's broken, and badly, shattered in two places. I fell through a sidewalk and my leg snapped like a stick."

"Terrible," was all Russell could offer. His throat was raw and scorched.

"Indeed," replied the gentleman. "I came out of my office and was nearly trampled. Then I broke my leg. I hopped a short distance then found the only crutch I could. This broken piece of a door. Quite unwieldly but there was nothing else." He smiled a little, as if embarrassed not to have a proper crutch.

"I can't help you walk," said Russell. "My hand's burned and useless. But we can get in the river on your door."

"Oh," said the gentleman, glancing back at the fire. "I can't swim!"

"The door will hold us up. Don't worry. I've crossed a river once already. You're with an expert."

"And if I slip off?"

"I can swim."

"With one hand?"

"Yes."

The man looked doubtful but it was clear from the trembling of his jaw that he was terrified of being left behind, terrified of dying. He nodded. Russell helped him to the edge of the retaining wall. Bracing with his elbow and knees, Russell lowered the gentleman into the water with the door. Then he slid down himself, grabbed onto the door with his good hand, and the two floated out toward the center of the river. Several bodies drifted past. On a makeshift raft nearby, a group of men sang a cheerful German song. The wakes of larger boats brushed them aside and they bobbed on the waves.

Russell paddled and kicked against the current of the river so they would not be drawn out into the lake, using his foot to push away from boats that came too close. They bobbed, clinging to the door as the terrible fire reached the river's edge, the gentleman too afraid to talk, Russell too weary and in too much pain.

This is a dream this is a nightmare this is not real this is so very real.

Each minute was an hour. Each hour a year.

Sometimes in the early morning, the fire jumped the river to North Division, and by daylight there were no more spectators on the north bank, only burning warehouses and wharves. The curious had fled.

The exhausted gentleman at last spoke. "When do you think it will be safe to get out of the river? My leg is numb."

Russell, his throat crackling and dry, said, "Not yet, I'm afraid."

"My name is George Rainey," said the gentleman. "I am a reporter with the *Chicago Tribune.* I dare say my office is nothing but cinders by now."

"I'm Russell Cosgrove," said Russell. "I'm a poor man who has tried in vain for months to raise money for my charitable home for the honest poor near Conley's Patch. I dare say there is nothing left there, either."

They floated for what seemed like many more hours as the smoke held low over their heads. They talked as Russell's aching legs worked mechanically, steadfastly, against the current. The sun, barely visible in the sky, moved overhead and down to the west.

At long last, Russell could see the people on their rafts work their way over to the south bank, and people on the wharves hauling them up. It was nearly dark, and although fires continued to burn in South Division, the worst seemed to be past. Those living in North Division had a long ordeal still ahead of them.

Russell shouted up to several policemen standing on a wharf. "Give us a hand!" Lying prone on the dock, one scorch-faced officer reached out and grabbed Russell by both arms. With a grunt and tug, the man hoisted Russell upward. Once on the wharf, Russell forced himself to stand, staring at some of the others who had been brought out of the water. Many were coughing, some were sitting and shaking. Others were dead, saved from the blaze but drowned in the river.

George Rainey was dragged up to the wharf with a lot of groaning, but Russell didn't wait to speak to the gentleman again. He would be fine, even with his broken leg. He was alive.

While most of the city was gone.

Russell hobbled to the end of the wharf, stepping over people, trying not to look at the fear in the eyes of the living and the vacancy in the eyes of the dead. To the south, there were still flames leaping above some structures while others smoldered. Buildings of all sizes and uses had been reduced to blackened rubble. The stench of devastation hung in the air. A tiny, soot-covered pony ran past, whinnying in terror, its harness flapping.

Russell stood at the river's edge and stared. He touched the red, crisp skin of his face and studied the curled, damaged fingers of his hand. Then he began to walk along the river, stepping around the injured and the dead, feeling a despair so heavy he was sure he would collapse beneath it. It was as if Hell had risen up from beneath the Earth to show humankind what it was like.

I'll never find her. And so, this is where I'm left. And somehow, I must start over. I don't know how.

He continued to walk. Every fiber cried out with grief and he put his hands to his face. Any tears he might cry were lodged painfully in his lungs.

This is my destiny? How can I even go on?

"Russell?"

I'm imagining that. I'm losing my mind.

"Russell?"

Russell stopped. He looked down at two women seated on the ground near him. A drenched, elderly woman was holding a drenched woman with yellow hair. The old woman's face was smeared with lip color and rouge. Hooked to the elbow of the younger woman was a brocade satchel. Several feet away stood a boy holding an angry, wet kitten in his arms. Lying prone in the dirt beside the boy was an auburn-haired woman in a torn, frilly dress. Russell knew the auburn hair, the dear face.

Katina?

"Russell?" repeated the old woman.

"Madame Jocelyn?"

"Russell!" Bruce cried, bounding to his side with the kitten and giving Russell a one-armed hug around the waist. "We thought you were dead!"

Katina!

Russell hugged Bruce back and then stepped around him, dropped to his knees, and scooped Katina up in a tight embrace. Her eyes didn't open. Her cold, soaked body didn't move.

"We thought you was burned alive!" said Bruce.

Russell rubbed Katina's face, her neck. He put his hand to her heart but felt nothing. "Katina?"

No, God, not this! Anything but this! To miraculously find her here, yet to find her gone?

He put her head in his lap and began to weep.

Not after all this!

He squeezed her close, wanting to take her into himself, to never let her go. To have and to hold. He held her tighter. Tighter.

Anything but this!

She moved slightly.

Russell's head shot up. She was looking at him with bleary eyes.

"Katina!"

"Russell," she whispered. "You're wet all over again."

"Yes."

"I thought…I thought you hated being in the river."

Russell laughed. He kissed the top of her head, rocked her, and laughed.

The sound was glorious on the dark and smoky Chicago wind.

21

Chicago Faces Inferno, and in Spite of Devastation, Hope and Charity Reign

At long last prayers were answered, and a torrent of blessed rain arrived late Monday night over the city of Chicago. The majority of the deadly fire was no longer burning by mid-Tuesday. The inferno raged an area four miles long and one mile wide. 17,500 buildings are destroyed, seventy-three miles of streets and walks are gone. Close to 300 people have been burned alive, crushed in falling buildings, jumped to their deaths, or drowned. 100,000 have been left homeless. Crosby's Opera House is destroyed, as were the Steward Grand Theatre and the Tribune building. This issue of the *Tribune* is being printed from a makeshift office in one small shop which did not burn completely to the ground, with scavenged ink and a donated press.

But there is hope in the aftermath, a spirit that rises higher than any smoke or flame ever could.

In the darkest hour of my life, I met a young man, unassuming and brave, named Russell Cosgrove. In the midst of the terrifying calamity that has befallen our city, Mr. Cosgrove, despite his own injuries, took pity on a stranger, helping him survive a night of hell on the river.

Charity has sprung up in Chicago, with donations

pouring in to help those devastated by the fire. Yet, I suggest strongly that Mr. Cosgrove be sought out, wherever he is. He chastised my heart without knowing it when he told me simply that he had worked for months, without success, to raise money for the honest poor around Conley's Patch. As a wellspring has been opened in oft-hardened hearts, I pray that those of wealth will take pity on our less fortunate brethren, that they will see them as Mr. Cosgrove sees them, not just during a tragedy but year-round.

For those who go without every day can be tragic, indeed.

George Rainey, *Chicago Tribune*
October 11, 1871

22

1891

October had been a particularly rainy month, with chilly breezes sweeping the city. Quincy Street was cobblestoned now, but rainwater still found ways to collect in low spots and send pedestrians to the street-side walkways. Telegraph wires had been joined by telephone wires, crisscrossing Chicago like a vast network of spiderwebs. Electric trolleys had replaced many of the horsecars.

Russell stood at the window of his apartment, looking out at the morning rain as it drenched the neighboring apartment buildings and drizzled down the window glass. He could see his reflection, lit by the gaslight burning over the desk behind him. Tall, dark hair, a trim beard obscuring much of the scar that had formed on his face from the burn he'd suffered long ago. One strong hand. One locked in paralysis.

"I wonder how much longer it's going to rain?" he asked.

The beautiful woman at the desk put down her pen and smiled. Russell turned from the window, letting the curtains fall back into place. On the floor beside the desk, two cats rolled about and played with each other, cats that were as lively and lovely as their great-grandmother had been.

"I remember saying once that I never wanted to see another raindrop," said Katina. Her auburn hair, now long and full, was swept up and pinned, with tiny curls at her cheeks. "Now I leave the weather up to itself."

"How is the play coming?"

"Oh," said Katina, glancing at the spread of pages on the desk. "This one is a bit difficult. But I think it'll be strong once it's finished."

"The audiences at the Steward Grand loved your last play. They've been clamoring for another."

Katina raised one eyebrow. At thirty-eight, she was more lovely than she was twenty years go. "I dreamed of fame and fortune as a playwright," she said with a laugh. "Back when I was a child with crazy ideas in my head. Yet here it is, with only a fair wage and not a soul recognizing me on the street. Except, of course, the Monroes from Michigan Avenue. Ever since my name was first mentioned in the *Tribune* as a playwright of some notice, they've been happy to invite me to tea regardless of their views of derelict Southerners. It irks me to have to call them cousins."

"But they've donated to Homeplace."

"Very little."

"Little is more than none."

"And done purely to look good in my eyes."

Russell chuckled. "For whatever reasons it was given, the money helps." He kissed the top of her hair. She smelled of love and joy.

The door to the study opened and a tall, handsome young man with auburn hair bounded through the door. "Father!" he said breathlessly. "Bruce and I were just now opening the door to Homeplace, getting the fire going in the stove, and setting out the books for the children's morning lessons, when a man rode up on his horse and handed me this envelope. He directed me to give it to you immediately."

Russell thanked his son, took the envelope, and opened it. It was yet another check, drawn on the Bank of Chicago, from the now-retired George Rainey. Ever since the fire, the man had taken it upon himself to collect donations of goods and cash from his wealthy friends twice a year for Homeplace. A new building had been constructed on the site where the old Stick Saloon had stood, with rooms for schooling and meals, and even a temporary shelter for women whose husbands were violent. Upstairs from Homeplace was a modest apartment in which lived Russell, Katina, and their eighteen-year-old son.

"Thank you, William," said Russell. "I'll be down in a minute. If the children come in and get rowdy, sing with them. You're always good at keeping order."

"Yes, sir," said William. He smiled at his mother and trotted off.

Russell put his hands on Katina's shoulders. She stood and circled his waist with her arms, putting her face against his chest. "The fire was horrific," she said. "Yet blossoms have arisen from the ashes. Charity and caring has grown in the hearts of some of our citizens. Much of life will never make clear sense to us, but as long as we see what is in front of us, and we appreciate and put to use what we learn, then we will be blessed. That is a gift."

Russell lifted her chin and looked into her eyes. "You are my gift."

Katina kissed him. He held her tightly, never wanting to let go. Then they walked to the window, clinging to each other, warm and safe, and watched the rain and the streets and the distant steeples and towers and the birds circling the air and flying out over the city to the sparkling lake to the east.

A Note from the Author

One dark night, when we were all in bed,
Lady O'Leary left a lantern in the shed,
And when the cow kicked it over, she winked her eye and said,
There'll be a hot time in the old town tonight!
– Folk song, author unknown

I've never lived in Chicago, but I have been fascinated with its people and history. Some of my best friends are Chicagoans, and they are fiercely loyal to their city and its works—from Lake Shore Drive to the Bulls to the sky-scraping Sears Tower. I wanted very much to write a book set in the Windy City during one of its most memorable, and devastating, historical events.

In the 1870s, Chicago was a city of growth and vision. As a metropolis on the frontier, it seemed just a little rougher and a little wilder than its eastern cousins such as Boston, New York and Baltimore. It was a bit of modern civilization raised from the swampy land beside Lake Michigan—determined, creative, and hardheaded. A town of less than 100 citizens in 1833, the city had grown in only thirty-eight years to a city of over 334,000. The citizens were proud of their modern fire-alarm network, their trained firefighters, and their up-to-date water system, which pumped water from the lake to hydrants all over town.

What really went wrong on the night of October 8, 1871? Chicago was used to fires; when not battling rain and mud, Chicagoans often endured long stretches of dry weather. The city was windy and most of it was built of wood. It was not shocking to read in the newspapers of a fire on the previous day claiming a home or factory. But how did this one get so dreadfully out of hand? Was someone to blame? Or was it just a terrible accident?

One thing was clear. The fires began in the barn of Catherine and Patrick O'Leary on De Koven Street. But in the 1870s, newspaper articles often read more like modern-day tabloids. Reporters didn't always check the sources of their information and sometimes even made up whole stories. While the fire did start at the O'Learys', it was reported by the *Chicago Evening Journal* that the O'Leary cow kicked over a lantern while Mrs. O'Leary was milking. The *Chicago Times* said that Mrs. O'Leary was an "old hag" of about seventy who had set the fire on purpose because she was no longer allowed to get county relief (an assistance to the poor) and wanted revenge against the city. None of this was true. Mrs. O'Leary was only in her thirties, had never been on county relief, and had been asleep when the fire began. However, the newspapers had given the city someone to blame and the woman suffered for it for the rest of her life. Cartoons were drawn, showing a witch-like Catherine milking her cow. Hordes of the curious came to their house to stare and harass. A postcard was even made and sold, showing a ragged old woman, posed as Catherine, with a cow and milk pail.

While to this day Catherine O'Leary is unjustly famous for starting the fire, there were other curious accusations. Some rumors blamed "Peg-Leg" Sullivan for setting the fire while drinking. There was even gossip that a fire extinguisher salesman, despondent because of poor sales, set the fire to show why his product was needed.

But why did the fire spread so quickly with so little resistance? Again, people wanted a scapegoat. Some accused firefighters of being drunk that night. Even the poor of the city had blame placed on them, with accusations that immigrants had slowed the progress of the firefighters by drifting along in the streets, in the way of the engines, rioting, and cursing.

An inquiry was held in Chicago in November of 1871. Many solid reasons were offered as to why the city burned so badly. These included the very dry weather, the strong winds, and the fact that so much wood was used in the construction of the houses, sidewalks, businesses, and roads. It was also pointed out that the fire department did not have enough men on staff, that an alarm was not turned in at Goll's drugstore, that there were not enough hydrants, and there was a lack of fireboats to patrol the river.

New building regulations were put into place after the Great Fire. Unfortunately, these required most of the buildings that had been destroyed to be rebuilt with stone or brick. Because most of the poor did not have fire insurance, they could not afford to do this. The division between the rich and poor grew wider as those without the means to build according to code were forced to rebuild their new, wood homes outside the city's commercial district. Justice-minded people like my fictional Russell Cosgrove and Katina Monroe would continue working hard to bring the plight of the poor to the wealthy. Other real-life activists such as Jane Addams and Ellen Gates Starr labored tirelessly in the late 1800s to assist the impoverished of Chicago. See "Hull House."

About the Author

Elizabeth Massie is a Scribe- and Bram Stoker Award-winning author of numerous novels and short stories, primarily in the horror and historical genres. She writes for adults as well as young adults and middle grade readers. Her novels, novelizations, and collections include *Sineater, Desper Hollow, Homeplace, Wire Mesh Mothers, Hell Gate, Madame Cruller's Couch and Other Dark and Bizarre Tales, It Watching, Sundown, Afraid, The Tudors: King Takes Queen, Versailles, Buffy the Vampire Slayer: Power of Persuasion,* the Young Founders series, the Ameri-Scares series, and more.

A former middle school science teacher, she now presents creative writing workshops to students in grades 3-12 as well as at the college level. She lives in the beautiful Shenandoah Valley with her mega-talented illustrator husband, Cortney Skinner. In her spare time, she likes to knit, geocache, travel, and sip a chai at Starbucks.

CROSSROAD
PRESS

Made in United States
North Haven, CT
10 March 2022

16983788R00100